RAINY-DAY DREAMS

Once inside the lobby, she went to the window that fronted on Albermarle Street and pushed aside the heavy drapery so she could watch Lord Crighton drive away. Large raindrops splashed against the glass, and outside the sky had grown dark as night. As for the curricle and pair, they were gone, and with them the most fascinating man Olivia had ever met.

David Crighton was a rogue, one who did things his own way, without thought for the danger involved. When she was with him, a bit of his daring seemed to creep into her very soul, making her say and do things that were totally unlike her usual self.

The thing was, she liked the way she felt when in his company. With him she felt free. Uninhibited.

But what of him? How did he feel? He had said he liked her eyes, but was that enough?

"Do you wish to see me again?" she asked beneath her breath.

Naturally, the gentleman did not hear the question, and the raindrops coursing down the window took no interest in the affairs of humans. Olivia was being foolish—she knew that. Even so, something inside her prayed that David Crighton would call upon her again. And soon.

The Secret Diary

Martha Kirkland

A SIGNET BOOK

SIGNET
Published by New American Library, a division of
Penguin Group (USA) Inc., 375 Hudson Street,
New York, New York 10014, U.S.A.
Penguin Books Ltd, 80 Strand,
London WC2R 0RL, England
Penguin Books Australia Ltd, 250 Camberwell Road,
Camberwell, Victoria 3124, Australia
Penguin Books Canada Ltd, 10 Alcorn Avenue,
Toronto, Ontario, Canada M4V 3B2
Penguin Books (N.Z.) Ltd, Cnr Rosedale and Airborne Roads,
Albany, Auckland 1310, New Zealand

Penguin Books Ltd, Registered Offices:
80 Strand, London WC2R 0RL, England

First published by Signet, an imprint of New American Library,
a division of Penguin Group (USA) Inc.

First Printing, June 2003
10 9 8 7 6 5 4 3 2 1

*To my favorite Web site guru, Rochelle Germain,
and to her newest creation, baby Tara.*

Chapter One

London, April 1814

*S*he saw him the moment she stepped inside the lobby of Grillon's Hotel, at number seven Albemarle Street. Grillon's was the premier hotel in London, the home away from home for ladies and gentlemen of quality as well as for visiting royalty, and it was rumored that interesting people might be found in the elegantly appointed lobby at almost any hour of the day. There was every reason to believe the rumor, for even though it was not yet noon, and most of the *ton* were still abed, the air in the hotel resonated with the dignified hum of numerous voices.

On some level, Olivia Mallory's mind registered the fact that hotel employees, as well as private servants in colorful livery, scurried about the ground-floor space, while here and there among the potted plants, handsomely dressed guests occupied the expensive settees and chairs, chatting with acquaintances. Yet she saw only him. And "interesting" did not begin to describe the man.

At first it was his eyes that held her, eyes the dark blue of a summer evening's sky, eyes that made her wonder if he had the power to hypnotize. Not that it mattered, for hypnosis was mere mind control, and something far more potent rendered Olivia unable to move. The man possessed some undeniably masculine power that strummed some hitherto unknown feminine chord inside her, making her ask herself what music she and the stranger might play together.

Embarrassed at such a wanton thought, she hurriedly replied to the greeting of the reed-thin concierge, who stood behind the mahogany desk, and took the ink-dipped quill he offered. After writing her and her sister's names in the guest book, she rocked the baize-covered hand blotter back and forth across the names to make certain the ink was dry.

The concierge studied the names, apparently having difficulty with the penmanship. Turning red as a radish, he said, "I am George Vickers. Miss . . . er, Mellon, is it?"

"Mallory. Miss Olivia Mallory."

"And Miss Esme Mallory," replied the lady's younger sister, "of St. Guilford, Suffolk."

Looking much relieved, Mr. Vickers smiled. "It is a pleasure to have you with us. As you requested in your letter, a suite has been reserved for a party of two and one lady's maid. And if there is anything I can do to make your stay more felicitous, I am at your service."

"Thank you, Mr. Vickers."

"Are your plans fixed, Miss Esme?" He asked the question of the younger lady, for he had lost the attention of the older one, who appeared interested in something near the staircase that gave access to the hotel's upper floors. "I ask merely because it is helpful if we at Grillon's know how long we may expect the pleasure of our guests' company."

"At least a fortnight," the young lady replied, her pretty face alight with excitement. "My sister has promised to show me all the most interesting sights in town before we return to our home."

"Excellent," Mr. Vickers said. Obviously feeling

that the niceties had been observed sufficiently, he added, "Again, please call upon me if I may be of any assistance to you during your sojourn."

Olivia had heard nothing of what the concierge said, for after placing the quill in his outstretched hand, she had turned to glance once again toward the beautiful polished oak staircase. The man was still there. Of course, she had known he would be, for though she had looked away for some moments, she had felt the warmth of his scrutiny and was certain he had continued to study her from beneath his thick dark brows.

His right elbow rested negligently against the newel post at the base of the wide staircase, and in his left hand he held a handsome beaver hat and a pair of leather driving gloves. His beautifully tailored clothes declared him to be a gentleman, from the elegantly tied neckcloth that peeked from beneath the lapels of his York tan coat, down to the soft leather Hessians worn over fawn-colored pantaloons. A gentleman's attire, to be sure, yet Olivia was not fooled. It was what lay hidden beneath the expertly cut clothes that shouted the true nature of the man.

He was a pirate. A rogue. A breaker of hearts.

Tall and well-built, he was as dangerous looking as any man Olivia had ever seen, and yet she had the most ridiculous desire to walk straight to him. It was as if some inner voice told her to stop before him, place her hand in his, and say, "I am here."

Fortunately, her sister saved her from committing such an egregious faux pas, for at just that moment Esme dropped her reticule. When she bent to retrieve it, Olivia nearly stepped on her fingers. "Have a care, Livvy! I am persuaded I shall need these fingers in the years to come."

Olivia glanced down at her sister, mumbled something that sounded vaguely apologetic, then returned her attention to the man beside the staircase. Almost as if he had known she would look at him again, he smiled, then inclined his head in the merest suggestion of a bow.

Olivia's breath caught in her throat. How . . . how dare he nod to her, as if they were acquainted. What effrontery! No gentleman would do such a thing. But, oh, how she wanted to nod back to him.

She had never met anyone like him, and if she possessed even a modicum of sense, she would do all within her power to maintain that status quo. She had only to notice the slightly jaded upturn of his beautifully chiseled lips to know the fellow ate naive country girls for breakfast. Country girls like her and Esme.

Not that Olivia was exactly a girl, not after having recently celebrated her twenty-fifth birthday. Still, owing to the unusual quietness of the life she had led these past seven years, she was almost as naive as Esme. Especially when it came to men like the blue-eyed rogue.

Recalling that she was now the sole protector of her beautiful nineteen-year-old sister, Olivia forced herself to turn away from that mesmerizing gaze and that rugged, not quite handsome face. As she did so, she reminded herself that she had come to town with a definite objective. "Tell me," she said, speaking to the concierge, "is there a Royal Poetry Society?"

"Poetry?"

The concierge, in an attempt to hide a seriously receding hairline, had taken great care in combing his few remaining locks over his pink scalp. Now, as if forgetting the intricacies of his coiffure, he scratched his head with the blunt end of the quill. Immediately called to his senses, he did his best to replace any disarranged hairs. Meanwhile, he explained rather hurriedly that he did not believe there was a Royal Poetry Society. "But I will endeavor to ascertain if there are any less exalted poetical societies in the area."

Still embarrassed, he snapped his fingers, a gesture that brought two of the hotel's liveried footmen hurrying forward. "James," he said, handing the tall servant a large metal key, "show the Misses Mallory to suite two hundred twelve. And you, Robert, see to their boxes. Miss Mallory's coach is . . ." He paused, allowing Olivia to supply the needed description.

"An antiquated black and yellow Berlin," she said, "guarded by two grooms and a scowling coachman whose temper matches his visage."

"I'll show him, Miss Livvy," Hepzebah Potter offered, "so John Coachman don't bite his head off."

The freckle-faced maid, though she admitted to having passed her thirtieth birthday, was keeping company with one of the grooms who had served as outriders. Because Olivia knew about their attachment, she offered no objection to the plan, assuming that Hepzebah wished to bid her swain a private farewell.

Turning to follow the first footman up the stairs to their suite, Olivia was disappointed to see that the rogue with the mesmerizing eyes had disappeared. The sigh she could not hide must have given her away, for Esme sent her a measuring look.

"Tell me immediately," the girl whispered, "before I expire of curiosity, are you acquainted with the gentleman who was just here?"

Olivia felt heat rush to her face. "Do not be a goose, Esme. I never saw him before in my life!"

"But he acted as if he knew you."

"Be that as it may, I do not know him."

Though disappointed, Esme did not give up hope. "It has been seven years since your come-out, and one cannot be expected to remember every person one meets. Perhaps you have merely forgotten him."

Forgotten those eyes? That face? Those shoulders? Not likely!

Much had changed in the thriving metropolis since

Olivia's unexpectedly brief introduction to society—a season that was cut short by the boating accident that claimed the lives of her parents. For one thing, London was even more crowded than she remembered, with more pedestrians, more conveyances, and more workmen's drays clogging the cobblestone streets. Time had dulled her memory of the bustle of people and the constant noise, and she had forgotten completely the coal soot that belched from the chimneys of businesses and town houses alike to rain down on the streets below.

The noise, the bustle, and the dirt Olivia might have forgotten, but she would have remembered a man like the dark-haired rogue.

"London is a big place," she said, embarrassment lending a sharpness to her voice, "and it is absurd to think that I would know a man like that. I pray you, let us not speak of it again."

Esme, though younger, was not one to suffer an unearned rebuke. "For heaven's sake, Livvy, I was in jest. Do not turn missish on me, for I could not bear it. Surely we have had enough of Puritan behavior to last us for a lifetime."

Reminded of the strict deportment required of them during the past seven years, conduct their uncle felt it his Christian duty to impose upon the females in his care, Olivia had the grace to blush. "Forgive me, Esme. Obviously, old habits are more difficult to break than I had expected."

Olivia and Esme would forever be grateful to their mother's older brother, who took them into his home without once pausing to consider the disruption two young females might cause in his ordered life. And yet, the sisters had sworn, following Raeford Frant's demise during the influenza epidemic that claimed him and his daughter, to eschew forever their uncle's unnecessary restrictions. "As for the man by the stairs,"

Olivia said, "I cannot be held responsible for his having smiled at me."

"Of course you cannot. But, oh, Livvy, was he not marvelous?"

Though Olivia was six years her sister's senior, and should have instructed her to control such romantic foolishness, she understood perfectly the cause for the younger girl's sigh. "He was quite interesting," she said.

"Interesting! Pshaw, a newspaper article on netting purses is interesting. That man was the living, breathing embodiment of the count in Maria Edgeworth's latest novel. So mysterious and so . . . so . . . *knowing*."

Esme had whispered the last word, then attempted to smother her giggles behind her gloved hand.

"*Knowing* he most certainly is," Olivia replied. She kept to herself her conviction that he was the sort who had tasted life to the fullest, without doubt savoring sensuality in all its forms.

"Should you happen to find yourself in company with such a man, Esme, I want your promise that you will give him the cut direct. If he should speak to you, do not reply. And if he should persist, show him your back."

Not the least subdued by this Uncle Raeford-like advice, the irrepressible young lady giggled again. "But what if I show him my back and he takes a fancy to it?"

"Esme! You minx!"

"Oh, Livvy, admit it. The man was deliciously wicked-looking. And far too intriguing to ignore. And if he walked up to us this very minute, I would be hard-pressed to turn my back on him."

Olivia was very much afraid that she shared her sister's opinion, but wanting to put an end to the conversation, she said, "Unless I miss my guess, the stranger is the epitome of that sort of man one is always cautioned against. Now, can we forget about him? After all, we came to town for a very particular reason, and making the acquaintance of wicked-looking gentlemen has no place in our plans."

Esme sighed. "Believe me, I have not forgotten our primary purpose in journeying from St. Guilford." As if to show her sister that she was ever mindful of the important nature of their plans, Esme lifted the portable desk she held by its ivory handle. One of their mother's favorite trinkets, the slim rosewood case with its double leather straps, could be flipped open, then the inverted top slid into a strengthening groove that made it an excellent writing surface. "Here are the poems, all quite safe. I have not let them out of my sight, and last evening when we stopped at the Blue Dove, I completed the second copy you wanted. Every last poem is now duplicated."

"Excellent! I know Mr. Phineas Quartermaine will be pleased."

Olivia chuckled, for when the publisher had replied by mail that he was interested in publishing Cousin Jane's poems, he had informed her that he would need a much clearer copy. "Obviously Mr. Quartermaine was not disposed to spare my feelings, for he told me in no uncertain terms that my penmanship was the worst it had ever been his misfortune to try to decipher."

"That I can believe."

"Esme!"

"I am sorry if the truth gives you pain, Livvy, but you must admit your penmanship is atrocious. Why, in my schoolroom days, when you wrote out my lesson assignments, there were times I was obliged to squint and strain until my eyes grew weak just trying to make out your ham-fisted scrawl. It is a wonder I ever learned the first thing about geography. And do not even mention sums, for even with Cousin Jane's help, half your numbers resembled nothing so much as the squiggly worms the grooms dug from the kitchen garden to bait their fishing poles."

Olivia might have defended herself against this oft-repeated animadversion had the footman not paused at the door to suite number two hundred twelve, on the second floor, and inserted a large brass key into the keyhole. When the door swung open, and Olivia got her first look at the suite, she could not hide her smile. The sitting room was a delight. Small, but charming, the room boasted cream walls, a rose velvet settee, and two blue brocade wing chairs. The two equally compact bedchambers were situated on either side of the sitting room, and a quick look to her left revealed the larger bedchamber, with its blue walls and counterpane.

"This one must be mine," Esme said, glancing into the chamber to the right, with its sunny yellow appointments, "for there is a trundle beneath the bed for Hepzebah. But, Livvy," she whispered, "this suite must be frightfully expensive."

"Frightfully," Olivia replied.

She had been shocked to discover that the suite she requested would cost the enormous sum of three pounds per day, for in a week's time the expenditure would come to more than dear Hepzebah's wages per annum. But what could they do? Nothing if they wished to stay in a respectable hotel. Fortunately, such an expense would not render them complete paupers.

Not for the first time, Olivia silently thanked her uncle for his kindness in supporting his two nieces for the past seven years. Raeford Frant had not been without faults, but never once had he made a demand upon the inheritance left the girls by their father. Instead, the money had been left to grow, untouched, in the exchange. For that reason, though neither sister was wealthy, they had more than enough income to allow them to live comfortably for the remainder of their lives. And, of course, Frant House, which had been unentailed, was now theirs.

As well, should Esme find herself wishful of marrying, there was sufficient money to supply her with a respectable dowry. Olivia doubted she would ever require a dowry. At her age, marriage was not at all likely; even though she had promised their neighbor, Mr. Vernon Sydney, that she would consider his very flattering proposal and give him her answer when she returned to Suffolk.

A truly worthy gentleman, Mr. Sydney had not approached Olivia until her six months of mourning for her uncle and her cousin were at an end. His petition for her hand and heart had been far from romantic, but because it was the first proposal she had ever received, and more than likely the only one she would ever receive, Olivia had been loath to refuse it out of hand.

Still, the prospect of becoming Mrs. Vernon Sydney, and spending the next fifty years of her life in quiet, respectable housewifery did not fill her with joy.

Olivia was a romantic by nature, and even her uncle Raeford's strict adherence to Puritan principles of behavior, which allowed for no social contact outside Sunday services, had not purged her of her love of music and dancing nor of her desire to fall in love. No more than the restrictiveness had kept shy, quiet Cousin Jane from falling in love, albeit with a man she knew only through correspondence and a mutual admiration of poetry.

"A Lament," one of Jane's poems, had explained that lady's actions so well.

> *Moments clothed in phantom shades*
> *A lifetime sadly wasted.*
> *In twilight's years shall I lament*
> *The wine I never tasted?*

Jane Frant was a thirty-six-year-old spinster, and had she not succumbed to a virulent case of influenza, it was likely she would have spent her expected three-score and ten beneath her father's roof. She would have dwindled into old age, forever known as Raeford Frant's dutiful, obedient, and unmarried daughter. Knowing this, Olivia did not judge her cousin too harshly, even though Jane's affair had been clandestine.

From their correspondence, it was clear to Olivia that Jane's admirer was a married man. He never came right out and acknowledged the fact, merely said he was not free to be more than Jane's devoted friend. Even so, Olivia could not fault her cousin for taking the crumbs of love that fell from another's table. Actually, had it not been for that clandestine love affair, and the poetry and correspondence her cousin had kept hidden in a false drawer in her bedchamber desk, Olivia might never have found the nerve to write to a publishing house, asking the editor to read some of her cousin's poems.

Olivia had hoped to honor Jane's memory by having one or two of her poems included in some future anthology. To her amazement, she received an enthusiastic reply from Mr. Phineas Quartermaine, who wished to publish all of Jane's poems in a single volume.

Dear, kind Jane. She had been so good to her two orphaned cousins. No mother could have been kinder, and now her one act of rebellion was the catalyst that sent the sisters on an exciting journey. They both craved a bit of excitement, and considering the quiet lives they had led these past seven years, Olivia was convinced they deserved a bit of diversion.

There were those in St. Guilford—Mr. Vernon Sydney among them—who advised Olivia to put the sale of the poems into the hands of some wiser head, which, of course, meant let a man handle the business. More than one villager told her to her face that a trip to town was an unsuitable journey for two unmarried females. Without the poems, and the needed excuse of conferring with the publisher, Olivia might not have had the nerve to ignore such nay-sayers. Thanks to Jane's silent rebellion, Olivia was now at Grillon's Hotel, and the lovely Esme had this unexpected opportunity to see London.

Olivia wished she might give Esme the benefit of a real *ton* season, but that was out of the question. Without a respectable matron to introduce her sister to society, such a come-out was impossible. Not that Esme had complained.

The girl had been wonderfully understanding. Far from complaining about the limitations of their upcoming journey, Esme had squealed with delight, then given her sister a hug that threatened to break several ribs. Without a moment's hesitation, she had agreed to be content with a fortnight of attending plays, visiting museums, and partaking of whatever delights London had to offer two single misses with only a maid to lend them propriety.

"Lord luv us!" that maid said now. Upon first entering the suite, Hepzebah Potter had stared in disbelief. "Would you look at the size of these rooms! Did I say rooms? Why they're no bigger than the larder off the Frant House kitchen."

"But such pretty larders," Esme said.

Hepzebah was not to be talked out of her growing disenchantment with London. "Dress a milch cow in silk, Miss Esme, and she'll still moo come milking time."

After a quick look around, followed by a series of *tsk-tsks*, the ever-practical maid gave it as her opinion that not a soul back in St. Guilford would believe her if she told them about this so-called suite. "No more than they'll believe the number of footmen standing idle in the hotel lobby, just waiting to run errands for the guests. As for the hundreds of people crowding the streets—dustmen and gentry alike—if I know aught of the matter, me pa'll accuse me of making the whole thing up."

"I might have suspected that someone had made up the entire story," said the soberly dressed individual who sat facing David Crighton, "had I not read the note and seen the evidence myself."

The gentlemen's smoking room at Grillon's Hotel, where the two men sat, was an oblong-shaped, masculine retreat, with its green leather wing chairs, its red flocked wall covering, and its teak wainscoting. At the moment the two men had the room to themselves, but if anyone had been near they would have been as surprised as the waiter by the disparity in the appearance of the two guests. David Crighton, the eighth Baron Crighton, was at his ease, with his long legs stretched forward carelessly and one booted ankle resting on the other, while the stocky individual sat upright, all business, appearing totally out of place in such an elegant setting.

Norman Upjohn, purposefully as nondescript as a little brown wren, seemed the very opposite of his roguish companion; and yet, the two men had much in common. For one thing, though they came from vastly different backgrounds, they had been similarly employed at the time of their introduction two years ago. Both had proven adept at gleaning facts others wished to keep secret, and each knew how to get in and out of potentially dangerous places without being detected. And, of course, they both spoke fluent French, though the brown wren's accent was that of the masses, while David Crighton's accent was that of the educated, upper-class Frenchman.

Anyone observing Lord Crighton at that moment might have been fooled into believing he was bored with the entire conversation—anyone other than the brown wren, who had reason to know what sort of man he was dealing with.

After taking a sip of the sherry supplied earlier by one of Grillon's waiters, Upjohn set the crystal wine-glass on the small teak table that separated him from the man who had requested his assistance. "Naturally," he continued, "the butler had thrown away the dead cat that arrived last month, but he'd saved the bandbox the creature was sent in and the noose that had been around the animal's neck. As for the funeral wreath that arrived in December, and the things that were sent in the past—something every quarter day for the last year and a half—those had all been discarded immediately upon receipt and never brought to your uncle's attention."

The man cleared his throat. "The butler had no reason to believe he was doing anything wrong in discarding them, for the items had been considered mere pranks—unpleasant, but nothing to become concerned about. First came a jar of lifeless bees. Next a hunk of meat with maggots crawling all over it. That sort of thing."

David took the news calmly, choosing to listen rather than react. "As you say, those items were unpleasant, but hardly threatening."

"No, sir. Not at first. Not until the box containing the dead cat arrived, with a note attached to the noose. The words of the note were cut from a newspaper, then pasted onto a sheet of common foolscap. Upon reading the words, the butler became concerned and showed the lot to Mr. Denholm Crighton."

"And the note said?"

"I didn't see it, you understand, but as near as the butler could remember, the sender accused Mr. Denholm Crighton of stealing something that belonged to him. And, according to the note, the time is drawing nigh when your uncle must pay for his crimes."

"Drawing nigh?"

"The exact words, sir."

"How very odd."

"My thoughts exactly," Upjohn said.

David replenished the wineglasses, more as a delaying tactic than a desire for more sherry, for he wanted to think. What sort of madman sent dead animals and threatening notes? And who in these modern times used such archaic phrases as "drawing nigh"?

Not for the first time, David wondered why his uncle had not apprised him of the threat. Had it not been for a letter he'd received a sennight ago from Mr. Paul Venable, his uncle's man of business, David would never have known of the sick jests. If jests they were.

Finally, David mentioned the subject he had been postponing. "In his letter, Mr. Venable gave it as his opinion that my uncle is suffering from a case of the melancholy. What have you to tell me of that?"

The brown wren looked down at his blunt-fingered hands, avoiding eye contact. "That sort of information is a bit trickier to substantiate, as I'm sure you'll understand, sir. I never cast eyes on Mr. Denholm Crighton, but even if I had, I'm no physician. I spoke only with the staff there at Grosvenor Square, and as one might expect of servants so long in the family's employ, they weren't what you'd call forthcoming when questioned about their employer's health."

"No, no. Of course not."

"All the butler would say was that your uncle had been a bit off his feed, as the saying goes, for about half a year. Eating like a bird, the servant said, and restless during the night, often remaining in his bookroom into the dawn hours. Not to mention refusing all social invitations."

"Half a year, you say?"

"Yes, sir. And since the dead cat and the attached note arrived just last month, it don't seem likely that either was the cause of Mr. Denholm Crighton's current despondency."

David remained quiet for some time, digesting the facts as presented to him by the man to whom he owed his life. "Thank you," he said. "I knew I could depend upon you to get to the truth without letting my uncle know he was a source of concern to his family."

David had been in town for a week, having come as soon as he received the letter from his uncle's man of business, but he had hesitated about going to the town house for a number of reasons, choosing instead to stay at his "set" at the Albany, on Piccadilly. The Grosvenor Square residence was legally his, being part of his inheritance from his father, but his uncle had resided there for twenty years or more. Since David was a bachelor, he had no need of so much space. Furthermore, he and his uncle were not close, and it was quite possible that he might view his nephew's concern as interference. Still, Denholm was his sole living relative, and David was concerned for his welfare.

His thoughts were interrupted by the arrival of the waiter, asking if he could get anything more for his lordship and his guest. David waved him off, but the brown wren took this as an opportunity to end the meeting. After swallowing the remaining sherry in his glass, he said, "I can have a man in the town house before sundown, sir. That is, if you'll agree to sending the present footman on a holiday while my man takes his place. I feel the circumstances warrant having someone in the house who knows how to handle himself in a crisis. As well, our best chance of discovering who sent the note may be to catch the person who delivers the next 'gift,' though I hope we can discover something before the June quarter day."

David did not hesitate with his reply. "Whatever you think best, Upjohn, do it, and send me the bill for all expenses."

He stood, as did the brown wren, and extended his hand in friendship. "Thank you, for your help. And thank you, as well, for agreeing to meet me at the hotel."

"Not at all, my lord. As it happens, I had errands to attend on Albemarle Street, so nothing could have been simpler." He took a look around him. "A handsome room, this. A far cry, if you recall, from that moldering hut outside Calais."

Actually, David remembered almost nothing of the hut or of Calais. He had been completely out of his head at the time, and as near death as made no difference.

He had spent several years in France, dedicated to doing his part to secure peace for his country, and during those years, his two most pressing objectives had been making reports to the Office of Foreign Affairs and staying alive. As it turned out, the former task proved far easier than the latter. In fact, in October of 1813, only days before the battle of Leipzig, the battle that led to the eventual fall of Napoleon's empire, David very nearly lost his life.

His true identity discovered, he was attacked from behind by a giant of a man who muttered, *"Vive l'Empereur!"* into his ear, then stabbed him in the chest and threw him into the Seine to drown. A watery death might have been David's fate had a river rat not pulled him from the murky waters. No hero, the thief robbed him of his clothes and his shoes, then left him on the riverbank, naked, seriously wounded, and friendless in a hostile land.

At least, David had thought he was friendless. Through a rather amazing stroke of good luck, he was found by the brown wren and taken to a place of safety. Unfortunately, that safe place, as well as the method Upjohn employed to get them back to England, was still a bit of a blur to David.

His recuperation required the better part of that

winter and spring. By the time he had finally regained his full health, men with his special talents were no longer required, for Napoleon had abdicated and was on his way to exile on the isle of Elba.

Since that time, David had remained on his estate in Kent, reacquainting himself with the land he had inherited on his father's death two years earlier, and enjoying the hard-won peace. Or he had been enjoying it until the arrival of the attorney's letter. As the new Lord Crighton, and the head of his family, he could not ignore Mr. Venable's concern for Denholm Crighton's health. Besides, it was time David had a taste of London society.

While he was in town, there was no reason why he could not renew a few old acquaintances; perhaps attend a party or two and flirt with all the pretty young matrons. If time allowed, he might even try to find a mistress—hopefully, one who would not bore him within two days' time. Though, to his surprise, the possibility of a new mistress did not appeal to him nearly as much as it had in past years.

What did appeal to him, more than he could say, was the possibility of making the acquaintance of the young woman who had met his glance earlier, the beauty with the luscious figure and the impudent gray eyes. He had looked at her, and she had looked back, without any of the missishness one might expect of a respectable young woman, and something—some mind-altering surge of energy—had passed between them. For the first time in months, David had felt totally alive. Not just lusting, but alive, with his senses telling him that something of real importance had just happened.

Before reaching the hotel entrance and venturing onto Albemarle Street, he took one last glance around Grillon's lobby, on the off chance that she might still be there. She was not, of course; that would have been too easy. Still, David Crighton was nothing if not adept at finding people, even those who did not wish to be found.

In this instance, the search should be relatively simple, for unless he missed his guess, the pretty girl with the honey blond hair and the perfect profile was the other one's sister, and she was just the right age to be making her come-out. All he need do was attend a few of the *ton* parties, keep his eyes open, and he was certain to encounter the beguiling miss who'd given him stare for stare without blinking.

Smiling at the prospect, he settled his beaver upon his head and strolled out into the afternoon sunshine, wondering if his old friends, Lord and Lady Selby, were participating in the whirl of parties that made up the London social season. David had not been in town long enough to receive any invitations, but he felt confident he could prevail upon the lovely Kitty to allow him to escort her to whichever of the numerous entertainments she meant to grace this evening.

With a flick of his wrist, he caught the attention of a passing hackney. "Cavendish Square," he told the jarvey, "and do not spare the horses."

As he climbed into the hay-strewn carriage, David grimaced at his own remark. Today was clearly his day for archaic phrases. There must be, he thought, a bit of leftover poet in him.

Chapter Two

By two of the clock that afternoon, Olivia had partaken of a light nuncheon, refreshed herself, then left Esme and Hepzebah to unpack the trunks and get the three of them settled into the suite. With a feeling of adventure, she stepped outside the hotel and asked the doorman to hail her a hackney, and only when he raised his eyebrows in surprise did she realize that her being unescorted would cause a stir. She had thought her age would allow her to move about freely, but it appeared she had misjudged the situation. Thankfully, the doorman hesitated only a moment before signaling the hired conveyance, then assisting Olivia into the carriage.

As the hackney traveled eastward on Piccadilly, Olivia stared out the carriage window, gawking like a first-time visitor to this city overflowing with humanity. It was so exciting to be back here, and since she knew from experience how quickly even the best-laid plans could change, this time she meant to enjoy the town to the fullest.

From Piccadilly the hackney continued up Shaftsbury until they reached Holburn, near the end of Leather Lane. Number eleven Holburn, a four-story codestone building of undistinguished architecture, was the home of Quartermaine Publishing. After exiting the hackney, then giving the jarvey two and six, which she was certain was nothing short of legalized highway robbery, Olivia entered the place of business and gave her name to a thin, sallow-faced clerk.

Minutes later she followed the unsmiling clerk up a flight of narrow, uncarpeted stairs, and at his sullenness, Olivia's spirits began to undergo a dampening. Was this to be her experience during her entire sojourn? To encounter nothing but disapproving males?

She got her answer the moment she entered the office of the publisher, Mr. Phineas Quartermaine. "My dear Miss Mallory," he said. "A pleasure to meet you at last."

Thank heaven! Finally someone seemed happy to see her. "A pleasure to meet you as well, Mr. Quartermaine."

The publisher was on the sunny side of sixty, with an inspiring mane of gray hair, and a more than substantial figure—one that probably rivaled that of the aging Prince Regent. When he rose from the wooden swivel chair behind his massive oak desk, the chair positively groaned with relief, and considering the publisher's girth, Olivia was not surprised at the noise. Phineas Quartermaine seemed not to notice the sound.

As he shook her hand, he smiled, a circumstance that might easily have led the unwary to mistake him for a genial person. Olivia was not misled. One look into the man's marble-black eyes was enough to warn her that if the publisher had ever come out on the wrong side of a bargain, the incident had happened too far in the past to be of any present significance.

"Do be seated," he said, pulling up a stiff-backed chair so uncomfortable it was guaranteed to put visitors in mind of other appointments. "May I offer you a cup of tea?"

Olivia declined the offer, and as soon as the large man reclaimed the chair behind his desk, and the groaning of the wood ceased, she got right to the point

of her visit. "As you requested, sir, I have brought
with me a much more legible copy of Jane Frant's
poems."

When the publisher remained silent, obviously waiting for Olivia to continue, she placed a thin leather
binder on the edge of the desk and untied the ribbons
that held the binder together. "As well," she said, "I
have brought the letter you sent me."

She removed the poems and the letter, then looked
at Mr. Quartermaine. "Though I am happier than I
can say, sir, that you liked my cousin's poems, I must
admit that I do not altogether understand your list of
requirements regarding their publication."

As if to refresh his memory, the publisher reached
across the desk and took his letter from Olivia's hand.
After perusing the contents, he said, "It seems perfectly clear to me. These are the basic criteria that
must be met before we can continue with our plans
to publish the book of poetry."

"I understand that, sir. It is the nature of those requirements that I do not compreh—"

"For the sake of argument, Miss Mallory, let us
agree that I know far more about the publishing business than you do."

Olivia felt her face grow warm, for though the remark was said in the most jovial of voices, she knew
a rebuke when she heard one. "Of course you do.
That goes without saying."

He nodded, as if happy to discover that she was not
a complete idiot. "That being true, madam, allow me
to tell you that a book of your cousin's poems—
charming though those creations may be—probably
would not sell enough copies to recoup our initial expenditure. Even if we went with the cheaper marble
board covers, I would be surprised if we made any
profit at all."

Now Olivia was truly confused. "It sounds to me,

sir, as if you mean to renege on your offer to publish
the poems."

"Not at all, dear lady. I merely wish you to understand that for the book to sell in quantities sufficient
to please both us and yourself, we must include at
least a few of Miss Frant's letters. The ones she received, and where possible, the ones she sent."

Olivia had never been interested in the earning potential of the poems, merely the fact that once printed
they would serve as a memorial to her cousin. She
had not meant to expose any part of Jane's private
life, other than her creativity, but she supposed she
could select a few letters that would not reveal too
much. "A letter or two might be possible, sir, but—"

"As I see it," Mr. Quartermaine continued, "the
book could be an instant success, perhaps rivaling the
first two cantos of Lord Byron's *Childe Harold's Pilgrimage*." He paused, giving that piece of information
time to register in her brain. "But only," he added,
"if we can show the mutual admiration that grew between your cousin and the gentleman. Naturally, to
do this we must include their correspondence. And,
of course," he said in a rather off-hand voice, as
though the matter were almost too trivial to mention,
"we should include a few of the gentleman's poems
as well."

"The gentleman's poems!"

Here was a development Olivia had not foreseen.
She felt light-headed and totally lacking control, like
a person being carried at breakneck speed by a run-
away horse.

The publisher remained silent, as if allowing her
time to gather her thoughts. Meanwhile, he leaned
back in his chair, with his pudgy fingers laced together
and resting on the middle button of a rather florid
waistcoat patterned in silver and green. If his pose was
meant to convey benign patience, it failed miserably,

for Olivia was reminded of a cat content to bide his time at a mouse hole, waiting for the eventual appearance of the rodent he means to make his next meal.

Feeling the need to explain her shock at his suggestion, she said, "Surely you do not propose that we include letters and poems written by a man who has no knowledge of their publication? Would that not be considered plagiarism? Or at the very least stealing?"

"Exactly so, dear lady, and I want no part in such a practice. Ours is, after all, a reputable publishing house."

"Then—"

He held up his hand to silence her. "You want your cousin's poems published, and I am more than eager to do so. Unfortunately, I do not believe the ladies and gentlemen who comprise the book-buying public are interested in another collection of poems by an unknown writer. On the other hand, the book I envision is just the sort of thing the public craves."

Due to her uncle's Puritan beliefs, nothing but religious literature had been allowed in Frant House. As a result, Olivia had not seen Lord Byron's poems, and it had been seven years since she had seen any other works of fiction. Even so, she had a niggling feeling that the sort of book the publisher proposed was better suited to the Minerva Press, where sensationalism was an expected by-product of the printed word.

Her disappointment must have shown on her face, for Phineas Quartermaine smiled. "You think about it, Miss Mallory. Take all the time you need. If you agree to my plan, I can guarantee you a book that is both tasteful and exciting, and one that will occupy a place in every fashionable drawing room in town."

He looked out into space, as if seeing something suspended there. "Two cantos," he whispered, giving the words a dramatic turn to rival the talent of Mr. Edmund Kean, the country's most gifted actor. "Each canto bound in handsome Morocco leather, with the edges trimmed in gold."

"M-Morocco?"

"Nothing less, dear lady. With perhaps a choice of blue or burgundy."

"Burgundy."

Olivia did not realize she had spoken. It was just that among the treasures hidden in the false drawer of her cousin's desk was a small diary bound in burgundy Morocco. Olivia had not yet allowed herself to look inside the diary, which was locked, but the fact of its binding seemed almost a message from Jane. After all, her cousin had chosen the diary. If Jane were here, would she choose to see her poems and letters similarly bound?

"I . . . I must have time to think, sir. Time to sort out my thoughts. See if I can determine what my cousin would have wanted me to do."

Mr. Phineas Quartermaine rose from his chair, signaling that the meeting was at an end. "I shall await your decision, Miss Mallory. But keep in mind that before I can even begin to sort through the material, I will require that you bring me written permission from the gentleman in question."

"I! But surely you have resources with which to—"

"Madam. I have a business to run. Besides, as heir to Miss Frant's worldly possessions, I am persuaded that you are the properest person to approach the gentleman."

"That may be so, Mr. Quartermaine. Unfortunately, I do not know where the gentleman lives. In fact, the letters sent by him are unsigned, so I do not even know his name."

"He already told you he did not know her name," Lord Selby said. The peer had only just crossed the figured carpet of his gold-and-white *salon doré*, to deliver a brandy to his old friend, David Crighton. Now he shook his head, as if apologizing for his wife's shaky grasp of the situation.

"Truth of the matter is, Kitty, my love, if he knew her name, I daresay he would never have offered to escort you to Lady Jessup's musicale. Dead bores, the Jessups, and I, for one, want no part of them or their caterwauling guests."

"Bores they may be," replied the pretty brunette who had the honor of being Lady Selby, "but their *ton* is excellent, and everybody and his wife will be there this evening." She turned to David, who had once figured as one of her beaux, and who was still one of her most valued friends. "If, as you suspect, this mysterious lady of yours is in town for her sister's come-out, then they will not miss the musicale."

Blowing a kiss to her husband, she bid him take himself to White's where he was bound for an evening of whist with several of his friends. "I shall do very nicely without you, Tristan." After looking David over from head to foot, taking in the corbeau green evening coat, the cream waistcoat, and the fern green knee breeches, she smiled. "Besides, to be seen in the company of a handsome peer who is destined to be pursued by all the matchmaking mamas cannot fail to raise my esteem among the *ton*."

Both gentlemen laughed, for from the first day of her come-out, the Honorable Katherine Windham, now Lady Selby, had been accepted everywhere, as much for her sparkling wit and general likability as for the indisputable wealth of her distinguished father, Viscount Windham. At twenty-seven, the brown-eyed brunette was still one of the handsomest women of the *ton*, and even though she had admitted to David that she was increasing, the high waist of the expensive rose satin dinner dress she wore hid all signs of the coming blessed event.

"Tell me, again," she said, "how I am to recognize this paragon of yours. You say she has blond hair?"

"Blond, for want of a better description," David replied. "There is a touch of red there, and you will know better than I what one calls the color. As for the younger one, her hair is a honey blond. And though I did not look at her for very long, I daresay the younger lady's eyes are green."

"She sounds an incomparable, and will probably be the hit of the season. But what of the one with the touch of red in her blond locks? Am I to understand that she is a beauty as well?"

When David thought about the matter, he decided she was more handsome than beautiful. Especially when compared to the younger one. Still, there was something about her that he found totally arresting, some quality that would have people turning to look at her long after her younger sister's conventional prettiness had faded.

"Her eyes are gray," he said. *Now there was an understatement of colossal proportion, for it omitted entirely the liveliness in the lady's silver-blue orbs, the enthusiasm for life and the spirit of adventure that shone from their depths.*

"Gray," Kitty repeated without real enthusiasm.

"Yes. This I know for a fact, for hers are the sort of eyes one remembers. And though the younger one has a cameo-perfect profile, I venture to say the older sister may have taken a tumble when she was a child, for her nose has a slight irregularity. Nothing to put one off however."

"No, no," Kitty replied. "Of course not. And when one considers the matter, perfection is definitely overrated."

"Though not," said the lady's husband, who was even then preparing to take his leave, "in your case, my dear, for you grow more beautiful by the day. Nay, by the hour."

Though the lady could not hide the flush of pleasure brought on by her husband's compliment, she bid him

leave at once, before he made a cake of himself and
her. The instant the drawing-room door closed behind
him, Kitty resumed her questioning of David. "What
more can you tell me of your lady? Is she tall? Short?"

"Of average height, I would say. As for her weight,
she is trim, though her figure is more than pleasing."

"If that is the case," Kitty Selby said, patting her
still flat midsection, "I am prepared to dislike her on
sight. For you must know, a lady who is increasing
should never be subjected to the totally demoralizing
vision of a lady who still retains her girlish figure."

Because the remark was too absurd to merit a reply,
David remained silent on the subject. After taking
only one sip of his brandy, he set the crystal snifter
on a nearby table and rose from the gold settee. He
bowed, then offered Kitty his hand to assist her to
stand. "Shall we go?"

"So early?" said the lady. "But it is only—" She
stopped herself in time, then looked up at her old
friend, a teasing smile on her lips. "My, my. I cannot
remember ever seeing a gentleman so eager to be
among the first guests to arrive at a musicale."

David returned her smile, though he had already
begun to wonder if he had made a mistake in confiding in her. "Surely you must know, Kitty, my dear,
that music is my life."

The lady had trouble maintaining her countenance.
"How foolish of me to have forgotten. Should anyone
ask me if I prefer Beethoven or Bach, I pray you will
allow me to refer them to you, my lord. The opinion
of a true music lover must always merit respect."

"Ah, respect," David said. "Now, there would be a
nice thing."

"Wouldn't it just," replied the lady.

After rising to her feet, she motioned toward the
rose velvet cloak that lay across the back of a gold
slipper chair, then turned so her escort could place
the wrap about her shoulders. "Our mutual love of

music notwithstanding, David, you find me positively consumed with curiosity to meet the unknown lady with the gray eyes and the reddish-blond hair."

As it turned out, her ladyship's curiosity was not to be satisfied that evening, for neither the lady with the pleasing figure nor the younger sister were among the guests at the Jessups' musicale. Worse yet, Kitty's husband had been in the right of it, the affair was a dead bore, with the term "caterwauling" being too complimentary for at least half the performers. More disappointed than he could say, David was delighted when Kitty said she was too tired to remain for the second half of the musicale.

"But do not abandon hope," she said, "for tomorrow evening Tristan and I are promised at Berkley Square, for a belated birthday party honoring Lady Sarah Jersey. Believe me, if your mysterious lady has a name, 'Silence' Jersey will know it!"

Totally unaware that she had been the subject of a hunt the evening before, Olivia slept the sleep of the just, then rose early the next morning, rested and ravenous. Happy to discover six covered dishes in the center of the small, round table in the sitting room, she served herself with toast, a basted egg, and a slice of ham. When she reached for the teapot, she noticed a note bearing her name propped against the cream pitcher.

Mr. Vickers, the concierge, had failed to locate the names of any poetic societies, but he suggested that she stop by Hatchard's Bookstore, at one eighty-seven Piccadilly, and ask there. Since Olivia had already made up her mind to procure a copy of *Childe Harold's Pilgrimage*, the suggestion could not have come at a better time.

"What say you?" she asked once her sister had filled her own plate. "Shall we stop in at Hatchard's before going to see the crown jewels?"

"The bookstore? Do you mean it?" Without waiting for an answer, Esme rushed on. "Let us go there by all means, for I wish to purchase a gift for Mrs. Blair. The only interesting books I have read this twelve-month—or ever, if the truth be known—were those I borrowed from the seamstress, then smuggled into the house. And though I am most grateful to the dear woman for sharing her treasures with me, I admit I should like to read something other than gothic romances."

"Oh?" Olivia said. "Let us hope that you had something a bit more elevating in mind."

"I had," replied the irrepressible miss. "*Modern* romances."

Knowing better than to engage in ineffectual discourse on the subject of her sister's taste in literature, Olivia enjoyed her breakfast, then went to her bedchamber to dress for their morning excursion. Having taken special notice of some of the ensembles worn by the ladies passing through Grillon's lobby yesterday, Olivia knew that hers and Esme's wardrobes were not the *dernier cri*, but thanks to the St. Guilford seamstress's skill in copying the styles shown in the ladies magazines, the sisters need not be ashamed of their clothing. Mrs. Blair's workmanship might not be the equal of that of Madame Claudette, mantua maker to the royal family, but the village seamstress was definitely skilled, and the materials she had used were as good as any found in England.

Confident that she would look what she was, a gentleman's daughter with a respectable income, Olivia donned a tan faille walking dress with a sleeved, three-quarter, russet pelisse, and a matching silk French hat adorned with cream and brown pansies. After freeing a few wispy curls to play against the turned back brim of the hat, and smiling at the effect in the looking glass above her dressing table, she returned to the sitting room to wait for her sister and Hepzebah Potter.

As usual, Esme was a picture to delight the senses. Her complexion, a true English rose, was rivaled only by the honey-blond curls that showed beneath her bonnet. Both the leaf green ribbons that tied beneath her chin and the velvet spencer were the exact color of her eyes, and for just an instant Olivia regretted anew her inability to give the beauty a real *ton* season. Not one to dwell overlong on circumstances that could not be changed, Olivia donned her gloves, slipped the large, brass door key into the inside pocket of her russet muff, then exited the suite.

As soon as they stepped outside the hotel, she had reason to be happy about choosing the muff, for the day was quite chilly.

"Brr," Esme said. "Will spring never get here?"

Olivia, with a show of sisterly affection, refrained from commenting on the chit's choice of lightweight clothing; instead, she kept her comments to the weather. "Such briskness cannot be surprising when one considers the severe winter the country was obliged to endure. Why, even old Mrs. Trusedale, who must be at least ninety, could not remember a colder winter, and according to the London papers, the Thames froze over completely."

"Lord luv us," Hepzebah said, "the entire river?"

"So the newspaper article said. The thickness of the ice was so great that on February first, a giant Frost Fair was held atop the river, with hundreds of booths and games erected for the entertainment of the citizenry. There were even musicians and enormous, colorful tents under which elegant suppers and dancing were available. If one is to believe the story, several thousand Londoners partook of the merriment."

"Wish we'd been here then, Miss Livvy. A fair like that would've been something worth seeing. Plus all them people walking on the water, so to speak. A bit of a miracle, you might say."

From what Olivia had read, the event was less miracle and more an instance of adventurers and would-be swindlers taking advantage of unlooked-for opportunities. And though she would be the last person to deny the citizens a chance for a bit of fun, she wondered how many pockets were picked, and how many cases of catarrh and putrid sore throat resulted in the time spent frolicking on the ice.

She said none of this, of course, merely stated that the extravaganza had been forced to close five days later, as the weight of the throngs in attendance had caused the ice to show definite cracks. "In the days that followed, I believe the sound of cracking ice could be heard for miles."

"You don't say so?" Hepzebah appeared lost in thought after that, obviously imagining the wonders of the Frost Fair, but as the three of them walked down Albemarle, then turned onto Piccadilly, Miss Esme Mallory was too well pleased with what she saw to wish for more. Frost Fairs were all well and good, but for a young lady who three days ago had never set foot outside Suffolk, just traversing the bustling streets of the capital city was excitement enough.

Every shop window drew one's attention, and if the displays were not sufficient to make one stare in wonder at the items for sale, the fashionably dressed ladies and gentlemen seen entering and exiting the shops were. In fact, these beautiful sophisticates were more than enough to make someone just up from the country gawk in amazement like the veriest bumpkin.

When they reached Hatchard's, with its entrance flanked by two small-paned bow windows, Esme removed the guidebook she had tucked into her reticule and read aloud the notation about the famous bookstore. " 'It was established by John Hatchard in 1797,' " she read, " 'with an initial investment of a mere five pounds. Its modest beginnings notwithstanding, the store soon became the premier literary emporium for ladies and gentlemen of discriminating taste.' " Looking up, she said, "I daresay they mean the *ton*."

"The *ton* and us," her sister added. "By any chance, did the guidebook mention the fact that the store is also a popular place for both planned and accidental meetings between young ladies and their gallant swains?"

Esme shook her head, though she was fascinated to be told such information. "But surely the young ladies are chaperoned."

"A minor point, to be sure, for the maids who accompany the young ladies either remain outside, occupying the benches set there for their benefit, or they congregate toward the rear of the establishment. As for the mamas, many of whom view any outing, no matter its purpose, as an opportunity for their marriageable daughters to be seen by potential husbands, they seat themselves at the tables set aside for reading."

Once they entered the store, Esme saw that her sister had described the situation accurately. Maids and mamas alike chatted with their own sort, while occasionally glancing toward their charges. Meanwhile, those charges, in their pretty pastel frocks and bonnets, progressed at a snail's pace up and down the bookshelf-lined walls. It seemed to be the thing to do, and when here and there a young lady paused to peruse the binding of a book, it was not surprising to see a gentleman "happen" past. Naturally, it would have been rude for the gentleman not to stop for a brief exchange of words, presumably to discuss the merits of whatever book had taken the young lady's fancy.

All this Esme took in at a glance, and though she followed her sister to a circular oak desk whose discreet brass overhead sign read PURCHASING AND IN-

FORMATION, her attention remained with the strollers. One in particular, a young man in an infantryman's scarlet tunic, claimed a goodly portion of her interest, for in her entire nineteen years she had never seen such a handsome gentleman.

Probably no more than three years her senior, he was fully six feet tall, with light brown hair and what she guessed were hazel eyes. Their color was difficult to determine, for the gentleman wore a black leather patch over his right eye. Not that the patch detracted from his goods looks. To the contrary. It lent them an air of mystery that caused Esme's heart to fairly leap from her chest.

The gentleman was noticeably slender, and in Esme's active imagination this circumstance was attributed to poor nutrition endured while proving his bravery on the battlefield. Slender, injured, and handsome. Surely he must be a war hero!

Whether or not he had actually achieved hero status, he was certainly well liked, for his progress was delayed many times by gentlemen who wished to shake his hand. It was while greeting one such fellow that he looked up and caught Esme staring at him. Naturally, she looked away, but not before their gazes had locked for a few seconds. And in that short span of time, Esme felt as if their souls had exchanged greetings.

"Excuse me," Esme heard her sister say to the bewhiskered clerk who stood inside the encircling information desk at Hatchard's, "but where will I find a copy of *Childe Harold's Pilgrimage*?"

"Permit me to show you," replied the man. He lifted the wooden apron that allowed him to step outside the polished oak circle, then motioned for Olivia to precede him. "Our poetry section is to your left."

While Olivia accompanied the clerk, Esme caught Hepzebah's arm, obliging the maid to remain where she was, in case she meant to follow Olivia. "Let us wait here," Esme said, for if she was not mistaken, the gentleman in the scarlet tunic was making his way toward them. If he came within two feet of her, Esme would need a chaperone, for she had every intention of dropping her reticule so that he could rescue it, thus allowing her to thank him for his kindness.

Dropping a handkerchief was, of course, much too obvious, but if a lady allowed the drawstrings of her reticule to slip off her wrist, who could say it was not an accident? Especially if her maid stood nearby to make certain nothing untoward occurred when the article was rescued.

Obviously, Hepzebah read Esme's mind, for she put her hand over the drawstrings to keep the reticule in place. "Here's a bit of good advice, Miss Esme, don't even think about it."

That was the trouble with servants who had known a person since she was in nappies, they never seemed to realize when the person was mature enough not to need correcting. "Think about what?"

"You know what, miss, and I'll thank you not to be playing off your country tricks here in this wicked city. I've got eyes in me head, and unless I miss me guess, this place is filled with half-pay officers and fortune hunters."

Half-pay officers! No. Not the war hero. Like a viciously sharp pin, Hepzebah's observation punctured the romantic bubble Esme had blown.

"You mark me words, miss, before your reticule hit the ground, there'd be a dozen ne'er-do-wells diving to catch it and use it as an excuse to force an introduction."

"But—"

"But me no buts, Miss Esme. You pull any of your tricks here in Lunnon, and it won't be me you'll have to answer to. Just let Miss Livvy get wind of what you're doing, and before you can say, 'Bob's your uncle,' she'll have you in a coach bound for St. Guilford, and well you know it."

Unable to deny the truth, Esme turned her back to the room and placed her hands and her reticule atop the wooden surface of the desk. She fancied she knew when the handsome soldier passed by, but she kept her hands motionless and her attention focused on a printed flyer announcing the coming of a new book by Walter Scott, the author of *Marmion* and *Lady of the Lake*.

"Shall I wrap them for you?" asked the clerk, who was even then returning with two leather-bound cantos.

"Please," Olivia replied. She stepped up to the desk, and while she removed a small leather coin purse from her muff, she asked the man if he knew of a poetry society that met in the area.

"Not right offhand, miss. But once I've seen to your purchases, there's a file containing the addresses of places where poetry readings and the like are open to the public. I'll be happy to check it for you."

Twenty minutes later, the helpful clerk gave her a piece of paper containing the addresses of two poetry societies, one where ladies were welcome at any time, the other where they were welcome only for the Thursday afternoon readings. After thanking him for delivering to Grillon's Hotel the Byron cantos, as well as the copy of *Marmion* Esme had purchased for Mrs. Blair, Olivia slipped the paper inside her muff. Moments later, she, Esme, and Hepzebah left the crowded bookseller's for the far more crowded thoroughfare of Piccadilly.

Fortnum & Mason's was just to their left if they wanted to take tea, and across the street and to their right were Burlington House and the Royal Academy, if they were of a mind to view the exquisite paintings housed there—paintings by such artists as Reynolds, Gainsborough, and Turner. Deciding to leave both those treats for another day, the ladies kept to their plan to view the crown jewels.

Because the jewels were housed in the Tower of London, which was on the other side of the city, they hailed a hackney and climbed aboard. Just as the carriage pulled away from the pavement, however, Olivia glanced out the window toward the forecourt of the building opposite Hatchard's. The Albany, with its central pediment and porch, was just as Olivia remembered, and she smiled to see that the brick-fronted building, which contained exclusive gentlemen's apartments, was unchanged.

In an instant the smile deserted her, for the entrance door opened and who should step out onto the porch but the mysterious blue-eyed man who had been in Grillon's lobby the day before. Afraid he might see her, and think she had followed him here, Olivia hurriedly moved away from the window, pressing her back to the squabs in an attempt to make herself invisible. In her haste, she poked her sister in the ribs.

"Livvy? For heaven's sake, have you taken leave of your senses?"

"It is him," she whispered, as if that explained her peculiar actions.

"Him? Who do you mean?"

Olivia attempted to push herself even farther into the squabs. "Did he see me?"

When Esme leaned forward to look out the window to see if the man had, indeed, seen anything, Olivia yanked her back. "Do not look!"

"Livvy, how am I to ascertain if he saw you, if I do not see him?"

As if to settle the question, Hepzebah stuck her head out the window and looked directly at the gentleman in the forecourt. He was, indeed, staring at the hackney as it traveled slowly down the street. "It's the gentleman from the lobby," she said. "You want I should wave to him, Miss Livvy?"

"No!" Her cheeks burning with embarrassment, she asked Hepzebah if the man was looking their way.

Apparently guessing what answer was required of her, the maid lied. "No, miss. The gentleman was looking in the opposite direction. I doubt he even noticed us. Common enough things, hackneys. Chances are Lunnoners don't pay them no mind."

Chapter Three

Olivia spent the entire carriage ride to the Tower berating herself. Only a complete ninnyhammer would have reacted so foolishly upon seeing the man again, and though she had been taken by surprise, she wished her sister had not witnessed the incident. How could she expect Esme to come to her for advice on proper behavior after the girl had been privy to such a freakish display?

Thankfully, she was not obliged to ask that question aloud, for once they reached the Tower, and the jarvey let them out near Traitor's Gate, on the banks of the Thames, Esme and Hepzebah were both too excited to think of anything else. Of course, Olivia was not unaffected herself, for as they passed through the gate, she felt a shiver skitter up her spine just thinking about the grim reception that must have awaited prisoners throughout the Tower's long history.

The Tower was begun in the eleventh century as a royal residence, though it no longer served in that capacity. It had gone through many changes, and now it contained the crown jewels, as well as a wild animal menagerie; even so, its history was ghoulish enough to satisfy even Hepzebah Potter.

As they paused on the green and looked about them, the maid gave a dramatic shudder. "Ooh. I fancy I can still hear the people cheering as poor Anne Boleyn's head fell into the swordsman's basket."

"Do not forget Lady Jane Gray," Esme said.

"She lost her head here too?"

"Oh, my, yes. Only her executioner wielded a heavy battle-ax." Esme pointed toward what she assumed was the Yeoman of the Guard's tower. "And up there, the Duke of Clarence died. Though not at the axman's hands. It is said the duke was drowned in a butt of malmsy wine."

"Drown, did he?" Hepzebah said. "Well, I'm sure that was a bad ending for his grace, but surely drowning's not as frightening as knowing there's a masked axman waiting on the green to relieve a person of his head? Only think of it, Miss Esme, how frightened Anne Boleyn must have been, forced to march to the chopping block, with the drums rolling and people gawking like it was a raree-show."

"At least," said one of the Yeomen of the Guards, who had just approached to inform them that a tour was about to begin, "each of the condemned got a brand-new chopping block, so they needn't put their neck against old blood."

The beefeater, as the guardsmen were sometimes called, looked splendid in his Tudor uniform. Obviously he had made that same remark about the chopping block numerous times, for when Hepzebah and Esme both shivered, he chuckled. Touching the bill of his porkpie hat, he apologized to Olivia, who had managed, somehow, to keep her reaction to the macabre fact to herself. "No offense meant, miss. It's the sort of thing most visitors like to hear."

Thankfully, before their imaginations got the better of them, they were joined by a group of a dozen or more people, and the tour began. Their initial stop was the White Tower, and by the time they left the first floor, Olivia had learned all she ever cared to know about crossbows, swords, and firearms. The crown jewels were, of course, a different matter, and all three of the Suffolk visitors were fascinated by the glittering array of crowns, bracelets, bejeweled swords of state, and royal scepters. Even without the gleam of all that gold, the timeless craftsmanship was enough to keep them *oohing* and *aahing* for hours.

They concluded their tour with a stop in at the royal menagerie, where lions and tigers paced back and forth in their narrow, iron-barred cages. When one of the beasts roared, several women screamed, and more than one child was taken outside sobbing with fear that the caged beast had just announced his plans for imminent escape.

For her part, Olivia felt sorry for the animals, and though it was exciting to see such beautiful beasts up close, she wished they had been left in their native environments. Since she seemed to be alone in her assessment of the situation, she kept her opinions to herself. No point in ruining the adventure for everyone else.

Still, she was more than happy to leave the wild animal enclosure, and once they were again outside, they strolled down to the river's edge for a glimpse of the numerous boats that traveled the Thames. After such an exciting day, it was no wonder that the three women from Suffolk were happy to take their evening meal in the seclusion of their suite, then retire early to their beds.

For about an hour after retiring, Olivia gave herself over to the adventures of Lord Byron's *Childe Harold*. Toward nine of the clock, however, her eyelids grew heavy, so she blew out her candle and snuggled down beneath the counterpane for a good night's sleep.

While the ladies in suite two hundred twelve followed their usual bucolic habit of an early bedtime, the ladies and gentlemen of the *ton* were only just leaving for the evening's round of parties. Among the distinguished party goers that evening were Lord and Lady Selby, and their friend, Lord Crighton.

Olivia Mallory was already fast asleep by the time Lord Selby's landau pulled up to the curb before number thirty-eight Berkeley Square, the London home of the fifth Earl of Jersey and his countess, the former Lady Sarah Fain. Candles shone in every window, and if the press of carriages was anything to judge by, the celebration of Sally Jersey's twenty-eighth birthday was destined to be one of the premier events of the season. And not just because her ladyship was one of the seven patronesses of Almack's.

It was true that a voucher from the countess all but guaranteed any young lady's social success, and for that reason the number of sycophants around her was incalculable. Even so, Sally Jersey was an extraordinary woman in her own right, and she was well liked. Her manners were sometimes less than genteel, and if she perceived a slight, she could be quite rude to the presumed slighter. And yet, it was a testament to her vivacious personality and her lack of conceit that she possessed a goodly number of true admirers.

David Crighton numbered among those admirers, so the blue-eyed gentleman was more than happy to figure as Kitty Selby's escort for the evening. Lord Selby was also in attendance, but as he had already declared his intention of going directly to the card room and not leaving it until his wife was ready to call for the carriage, Lady Selby was pleased to have a gentleman in reserve. Even if that gentleman was there primarily to search for another lady.

"Lord Crighton," the Earl of Jersey said, offering the newcomer his hand, "so nice of you to come."

"Especially since you were not on the guest list," added his countess, whose flirtatious smile gave the lie to her reproachful words.

"Lovely Sally," David said, bowing over the lady's

hand, "how could I miss your birthday celebration? After all, it is not every day that a lady turns twenty-one."

The younger Lady Jersey, disregarding the censorious looks being sent her way by her famous mama-in-law, rapped David's knuckles with her fan. "Flatterer," she said. "Be so good as to save your blandishments for someone naive enough to believe them, for I warn you I can spot a person in want of a favor a mile away."

David chuckled. It was one of Sally's charms that she seldom put on the sort of airs one might expect of a lady of her wealth and social position. "I have no doubt of your ability to discern those who would ask a favor of you, lovely lady, but in this instance, I guarantee I want only a name. And because you know everyone worth knowing, I hoped . . ."

The remark was left hanging, the line of guests behind them was growing, and proper etiquette required that they move along to allow others to be greeted. Still, from the smile Lady Jersey gave him, David knew she meant to help him if she could. Unfortunately, when he claimed her for the supper dance later that evening, she confessed to knowing no more of the young ladies he described than had Kitty.

"A strawberry blonde with a younger sister," Lady Jersey repeated, her fan pressed against her silken cheek as if it aided the thought processes. "There was a young lady with that color hair a season or two past, a Miss Bascum, I believe, but I can recall no one of that description this year. Are you sure, Crighton, that the ladies are here for the season, and not for some more serious purpose?"

"I am sure of nothing, ma'am, except that I am at a standstill. If, as you say, none of the socially acceptable matrons has applied for vouchers on the sisters' behalf, I begin to suspect that their purpose in coming to town was something other than frivolity."

In this he was correct, for the next morning Olivia lost no time in getting down to the business of discovering the name of the man who had exchanged poems with her cousin, Jane Frant. As it happened, the two poetry societies where she meant to begin her search were located no great distance apart, with one situated in the middle of Carnaby Street, on the floor above a tobacconist's shop, and the other found at the far end of Lexington Street, in a private home that had been converted to gentlemen's rooms some twenty years ago.

At the former, though the sign in the window declared that ladies were welcome, Olivia received a cool reception. "I am sorry," said a Mr. Wayrand, the secretary of the society, who appeared more irritated than sorry, "but I could not possibly identify a gentleman by his poetry alone, even had I the time and inclination for such foolishness."

As if much put upon, he said to no one in particular that next those of the distaff gender would be instituting hunts for mare's nests. "Or heaven forbid," he added with a shudder, "they will be bombarding us with demands to have their own pathetic little poems read aloud, to the embarrassment of themselves and the total boredom of the true poet."

Olivia was obliged to bite her tongue to keep from giving the man a piece of "distaff" advice as to how he might improve his manners. Remembering that the *true* evaluation of her worth lay in her own hands, and not with some dyspeptic little man, she contained her annoyance. After bidding the secretary farewell, she exited through the tobacconist's shop and took herself to Lexington Street.

Her reception was more felicitous at the second poetry society; even though it was Wednesday, and a discreet placard just above the door declared that ladies were welcome only during the Thursday afternoon readings, which were open to the public. With great forbearance, the president of the society, Sir Arthur Hix, invited Olivia to be seated at one of the half-dozen refectory tables crowded into the ground-floor meeting room.

The baronet was a short, rather effete man in his late forties. His graying locks were combed forward in a longish Brutus, and instead of a cravat he wore a spotted Belcher handkerchief tied around his neck. He looked every inch the poet, albeit an aging one. And Olivia disliked him on the spot.

Perhaps it was her previous experience on Carnaby Street, or perhaps it was the baronet's overrefined manner. Whatever the reason, she wished she did not have to ask the gentleman for a favor.

With the graceful movements of a dancing master—movements Olivia fancied he had practiced before his mirror—the president of the society took the sheet of vellum she offered, then raised a beribboned quizzing glass to his eye. After reading through to the last line of the poem, he shook his head.

"On such short notice, Miss Mallory, I fear I can be of little assistance to you in your quest. However, if you would care to leave some of the poems with me, so that I could study them at my leisure, it is possible that I might discover some rhyme pattern or a repetition of meter that would lead me to the poet's identity. I am a poet myself, you understand, so recognizing another's style might not be all that difficult."

She felt certain he mentioned his own writings so that she would ask if he had been published, and if so, where she might purchase some of his work. She could not bring herself to be so dishonest, for the last thing she wanted was to be privy to this pretentious little man's innermost thoughts. Instead, she thanked him for offering to read the poems. "You are very kind, Sir Arthur, but these are my only copies, and at this time I dare not let them out of my sight."

"Of course, I understand perfectly."

From the flicker of annoyance in his washed-out
blue eyes, he was insulted by her reluctance to leave
the poems in his care; almost as if she suspected he
might copy them for his own use. He said nothing,
however, merely cleared his throat, raised the quizzing
glass once again, and read aloud "The Journey," the
short poem he still held.

> *I am alone and far from home,*
> *Distanced from that place where*
>   *the river meets the sea,*
> *Adrift between gray ocean and*
>   *even grayer sky.*
> *I am too long among strangers,*
> *Alone, without my beloved, who sings*
>   *the songs I yearn to hear.*

"The author is not without talent," Sir Arthur said,
"but these few lines are insufficient to reveal to me
his identity. Assuming, of course, that I have ever seen
his work before. Is he published, do you think?"

"As to that, I have not the least idea."

Olivia had risen to take her leave when Sir Arthur
asked her if she had no clue as to the author's identity.
"Something that would give us a lead."

The idea of there being an "us" actually caused
gooseflesh on Olivia's arms. "Nothing, sir."

"Perhaps, dear lady, you know something without
realizing it. Among your cousin's correspondence is
there a return direction? Or a nom de plume? An
initial, even one, would be helpful."

"I have searched through every poem and every
letter, many times in fact, and there are no hidden
clues."

The moment the words were spoken, she recalled
her cousin's diary. The handsome, Morocco-bound
book was locked for a reason, so that Jane's private
thoughts and emotions could remain just that—pri-

vate. Naturally, Olivia had been loath to trespass upon her cousin's innermost secrets, but it was clear that if she was ever to discover any information about the man Jane Frant had loved, her only hope of doing so lay within the pages of the diary.

"Excuse me," she said, reclaiming the poem Sir Arthur still held, and returning it to the inner pocket of her muff, "but I just had an idea. One I must investigate."

The baronet saw her to the door, and as she exited the society's meeting room, he bid her return if she discovered anything pertinent. "I have rooms on the third floor, Miss Mallory, so I am here most days, and I shall be most happy to be of assistance to you in your search. Poetry is, after all, my raison d'être. My very reason for living. And there is nothing I would not do to further its cause."

Or your own! Olivia had no notion from whence such an idea had sprung, but once she was outside the Livingston Street building, with the baronet's pale blue eyes no longer watching her every move, she breathed easier. What maggot, she wondered, had gotten into her brain to cause her to feel such aversion to the prissy little man. After all, what harm could the would-be Byron possibly do her?

Chapter Four

"*I* regret the fact that I cannot oblige you in this, my lord," Mr. Vickers, the concierge, said, "but it is against Grillon's policy to reveal the names of our guests. I should be quite happy, however, to deliver your card, or a note to the Misses Ma . . . er, to the ladies."

Flushed with embarrassment at his near gaff, Mr. Vickers pointed to a doorway just off the lobby. "The reading room is over there, sir, if you care to compose a message to one or other of the ladies."

"Thank you," David said, "perhaps some other time."

Turning his back on the concierge, David asked himself what the dickens he was doing here, seeking information of a hotel employee and behaving like some moonling suffering from his first infatuation. He was thirty-one years old, for heaven's sake, and it was time he started acting like it. And yet, those expressive gray eyes and that intriguing smile seemed permanently etched in his mind. So much so that he had imagined he saw her driving away from Hatchard's the day before, and it was all he could do not to hail a hackney and follow her to her destination.

Too bad the concierge had slipped only enough to say the first syllable of her name, for it could be any-

thing. Miss Madison. Miss Madrigal. Miss MacHenry.
The possibilities were endless. Still, even those first
two letters were a start. While working for the Office
of Foreign Affairs, David had often begun a search
with much less information, and in those instances the
stakes were far more serious. At least his life did not
depend on discovering this name.

Be that as it may, some sixth sense told him that it
was of prime importance that he find an acceptable
way to meet the lady. If he did not, that sense told
him, he would regret it for the remainder of his days.

Abandoning the search for the moment only, he
went outside, where one of the hotel's footmen held
the reins of a pair of handsome matched chestnuts.
After climbing aboard the dark green curricle, with its
black leather upholstery and gold trim, David tossed
the footman a shilling, then gave the restive chestnuts
the office to be on their way. It was time and more
that he stopped in at Grosvenor Square to call upon
his uncle and aunt, and now was as good a time as any.

The few blocks were covered in a matter of minutes,
and when David arrived at the town house, he was
greeted by a servant he had never seen before. "Good
day," he said.

"Good day to you, sir."

Clearly this tall, rather muscular-looking fellow was
the man Norman Upjohn had put in place to protect
Denholm Crighton, and David was pleased to have
the opportunity for a few moments' private conversation. After handing over his hat and gloves, he asked
the fellow his name.

"I am Joseph, my lord."

"You know who I am, then?"

"I do, my lord, and if you will forgive the liberty, I
daresay Mr. and Mrs. Crighton will be happy to see
you. Especially when one considers how quiet it's been
here in Grosvenor Square these past few days."

Accepting the message that there had been no further contact from the person who sent the dead cat, David nodded. "Anything else?"

"Well, sir . . ."

"Have you discovered something?"

"As to that, my lord, I have and I haven't."

"Damnation, man. Out with it."

The substitute footman lowered his voice. "Last night, my lord, I heard something in Mr. Crighton's bookroom, and believing the gentleman had already gone up to his bedchamber, I went into the bookroom to investigate. Your uncle was there, my lord. He had been drinking rather heavily and was now asleep at his desk."

"And you found that significant?"

"I did, sir, because in his hand he held several sheets of yellowed paper. Letters, actually."

"Sent through the post?"

"Yes, sir. Four, to be exact, all bearing London stamps. However, I do not believe they were from the same malefactor as sent the dead cat."

David did not question the man's conclusion. If he worked for Norman Upjohn, he would know his job. Nor did he bother asking if the man had read the letters. "What did they say?"

"Each contained just one word, my lord, printed in crude block letters, as though the writer had used his other hand for the writing."

"And that word?"

"It was 'adulterer,' sir."

Adulterer! Surely the accusation was a mistake, for if there had ever been a man less likely to form a sexual liaison, it was Denholm Crighton. The man was quiet, bookish. A dreamer. As far as David knew, his uncle had never been a lady's man, not even in his youth, and when at the age of twenty-five he had been pressured by his father to marry, he had taken the course of least resistance and become engaged to the daughter of their closest neighbor, a plain, rather shy young lady he had known all his life.

And yet, what did one ever really know about another person? Perhaps the dreamer had taken his head out of his books long enough to notice another woman.

The note that had been tied around the dead cat's neck had accused David's uncle of stealing something that belonged to the sender of the cat, and it warned his uncle that he must pay for his crimes. Had Denholm Crighton stolen another man's wife? He certainly would not be the first of his sex to stray from his marital vows, though such "thefts" usually were settled with pistols, not dead cats and threats.

More concerned than ever, David gave himself a minute to absorb this new information, then he allowed the substitute footman to take him to his uncle.

Denholm Crighton sat behind a mahogany kneehole desk, a quill in hand, but at sight of his nephew, he gave a smile of genuine pleasure. "David, my boy, what a surprise to see you."

"Not an unpleasant one, I hope."

His uncle set aside his quill, rose from the desk, and traveled the length of the handsomely paneled bookroom to give his nephew's hand a firm squeeze. "Unpleasant? No, no, my boy. Not at all."

"Not in the least," Augusta Crighton added.

Denholm's wife had only just stepped into the room, obviously having taken a turn in the small rear garden, and now, after closing the French windows behind her, she crossed the room to place a chaste kiss on her nephew's cheek. "It is always a pleasure to see you, David. Though I am quite curious as to what has brought you up from Kent."

Not wanting to mention anything about the dead cat incident, on the chance that his uncle had chosen not to inform his wife, David said the first thing that came to mind. "I attended Lady Jersey's birthday celebration last evening. And what a gala it was. A regular crush, with all the world and his wife in attendance, and the dowager Lady Jersey watching her daughter-in-law like a hawk, as if hoping to find some fault with which to berate her later."

His aunt accepted the "misused" truth without question, apparently eager to hear any news of society. "And what of the dowager's illustrious cicisbeo?" she asked. "Was His Royal Highness in attendance?"

"Prinny? Not while I was there, ma'am. So the older Lady Jersey was obliged to make do with one of her less exalted admirers."

It was not a new joke, but his uncle and aunt both smiled in appreciation. "I had thought to see you both there, but apparently you had some more pressing engagement."

His uncle motioned David to one of the overstuffed wing chairs that flanked the fireplace, while he resumed his place behind the desk. "Actually, Augusta and I do not go out much these days."

"Oh? And why is that? Never tell me you have become a recluse."

This time his uncle's smile was a bit strained. "No, no. Nothing like that. We are, however, much more selective these days as to what invitations we accept." The words sounded cheerful enough, but the older man's eyes held a sadness David had never seen in them before. As well, his uncle looked much older than he had last time they had met.

Denholm Crighton was only forty-eight years old, and his wife was still on the sunny side of forty-five, and yet, they had both aged beyond their years. There were dark circles beneath his uncle's eyes, attesting to his lack of sleep, and he appeared jumpy, his nerves taut. Also, Denholm had lost a noticeable amount of weight that, along with his sad countenance, supported the concerns of his man of business that he suffered from some sort of melancholy.

David wished he could broach the subject of what was disturbing his only relative, but he knew better than to give his uncle cause to snub him. Instead, he said, "I hope, sir, that your newfound selectivity will not oblige you to refuse an offer I wish to extend to you and my aunt for this evening. I have hired a box at Covent Garden, and I shall be quite disappointed if you refuse to accompany me."

"Covent Garden," Augusta Crighton said, not even attempting to hide the wistfulness in her voice. "What a treat, is it not, Denholm? For you have always loved the theater."

His uncle said nothing.

"The drama is *Richard III*," David added, "and if memory serves, that is your favorite of the Shakespeare histories."

"Famous," Augusta said, her voice edgy, a bit too bright. "We should love it, should we not, my dear?"

"Some other time," Denholm Crighton said. "Take your aunt, by all means, my boy. As for me, pray excuse me, for I have a previous engagement."

David looked from his aunt's disappointed face to the lackluster countenance of his uncle. "Please, Uncle, could you not make some sort of excuse that would release you from your previous commitment? We are still a family, after all, and it has been years since we—"

"Denholm, please," August begged, her voice watery with unshed tears. "Just this once. Surely you can spare one evening to—"

"I cannot go! Must you be forever hounding a man?"

His sharp reply having put an end to his wife's supplication, Denholm rose from the desk and hurried through the French windows, out into the narrow back garden.

Silence reigned for several minutes, with nothing filling the void but the muffled sound of Augusta's weeping. "Your pardon," she said at last, pressing a linen handkerchief to her tear-streaked cheeks. "I seem to have turned into a watery pot the last few months."

"No apology needed, ma'am."

While his aunt wiped away the last of her tears, David asked if she had any objections to his stopping back by tomorrow to see his uncle.

"Please do. Perhaps he will confide in you the reason for this newfound reclusiveness."

David hoped that would be the case, but he did not wish to push for confidences. "In the meantime, ma'am, I see no reason why you and I should not take advantage of the box I hired."

"Oh, no. Really, I could not. What would Denholm say?"

"I believe my uncle has already said it. He does not wish to go. All that remains is for you to say what you wish to do. For my sake, I hope it is that you will allow me the pleasure of your company."

She hesitated only a moment, then nodded. "I should like to go."

"Excellent. Shall I call for you this evening at half past seven?"

Olivia's excursions to the poetry societies had been both fruitless and unpleasant, so she said very little about the experiences, merely that she had not met with success. Esme said everything that was sympathetic, but she soon changed the subject to the promised afternoon outing, which included a visit to view the famous Elgin Marbles. "Are you too done in for a bit of Greek culture?"

"Not at all," Olivia said. "A cup of tea and I shall be my old self."

Actually, she was happy to agree to do anything that would rid her thoughts of Sir Arthur Hix. As well, she did not relish carrying out her proposed invasion of Jane's diary. Reasoning that a few hours could not make all that much difference in the grand scheme of things, she promised herself she would begin her search of the diary that evening without delay. She had given her word that she would show her sister the town, and that promise was every bit as important as discovering a clue to the identity of Jane's poet-lover.

Olivia had never seen the famous Elgin Marbles, and upon viewing the Greek antiquities for the first time, her feelings were similar to those she had experienced while viewing the wild animals at the Tower menagerie. The marbles were beautiful, and it sparked her imagination to be so close to something of such artistic and historical value. She did wonder, however, if it would not have been better to have left the marbles at the Parthenon, from whence they had been taken. Greece was their home, after all, not England.

For the past six years, Lord Elgin had displayed the marbles in a rough sort of portico attached to his town house, but viewing the treasures was possible for almost anyone who dressed and behaved in a respectable manner. Olivia, guessing rightly that Hepzebah would not appreciate the educational exhibit, had brought only Esme to view the Grecian wonders. Now, having traveled the length of the portico and having observed each of the antiquities from every possible angle, the sisters left the enclosure.

"How would you feel," Olivia asked, continuing her argument against removing treasures from their native land, "if a team of Greek explorers landed in London and helped themselves to a few of the crowns and scepters we saw yesterday at the Tower?"

"Come now, Livvy, the circumstances are hardly the same."

"I beg to differ. I think they are very much the same. The items in the Tower belong to Britain, while the decorations of the Parthenon belong to Greece. For my part, I cannot see that there is any other possible view of the matter."

"But—" Esme ended the argument on the spot, for she had spied a young matron stylishly attired in a pomona green carriage dress with a matching pelisse and a jaunty little bonnet. Unfortunately, the lady herself looked far from jaunty, for she sat on one of the stone benches in Lord Elgin's side garden, and unless Esme was very much mistaken, the lady was in distress. "Livvy, look over there, on the bench. I am persuaded the lady with the handkerchief to her lips is in danger of fainting."

"In this cool weather? I hardly think that at all likely."

Though she assumed that Esme had misread the situation, Olivia looked toward the stone bench, and as her sister had said, the lady did, indeed, look to be in distress. A very pretty silk parasol lay on the ground, all but forgotten beside her elegantly booted feet, and the lady was drawing in deep breaths, as if hoping to ward off an attack of dizziness or nausea. Because the young woman was alone, without a maid or escort of any kind, Olivia did not hesitate, but walked forward purposefully, with Esme following close behind.

"Excuse me, ma'am," Olivia said, "but may I be of any assistance to you?"

The young matron looked up, and though she tried to smile, her face was unusually pale, and tears had pooled in her large brown eyes. "My brother has gone to fetch our carriage, but I— Oh. Ohh! Forgive me, but I think I am about to be unwell." The words had no more than left her lips when a wave a nausea forced the young woman to turn and cast up her accounts on the far side of the bench.

"You poor thing," Olivia said, holding the lady's

shoulders so she need not fear toppling over. Once
the wave of nausea had passed, she asked her if she
had any sal volatile. The lady merely pushed her reticule into Olivia's hands.

"Esme, you look."

Esme took the reticule, and within moments she
had found the vial of spirits, removed the cap, and
begun waving the smelling salts beneath the young
woman's nose. Whether it was the sharp aroma of the
sal volatile, or the fact that the poor lady had nothing
left to cast up, she began to rally almost immediately.

"I . . . I am so embarrassed."

"Nonsense," Olivia said, "it could happen to anyone." She seated herself beside the lady in green, and
after putting her arm around the slender shoulders,
guided the jockey bonnet and glossy black curls down
to her own shoulder. "Rest against me, ma'am. I am
persuaded you will feel much more the thing if you
simply give in to the moment and allow me to be
of assistance."

The lady was too ill to stand on ceremony, so she
rested her head against Olivia's shoulder for about a
minute. Then, as if needing to explain her behavior,
she whispered that she was in an interesting condition.
"But this is the first time I have made a spectacle of
myself in public."

"Nothing of the kind, I assure you. And may I offer
you my congratulations?"

"Thank you. And thank you as well, for being so—"
The lady in green had straightened, and now she
looked Olivia directly in the face. "Pardon me, but do
I know you?"

It was Olivia's turn to study the still wan countenance so close to hers, and though she could understand why the lady had not immediately recognized
her, she was almost embarrassed not to have recognized the Honorable Katherine Windham. Kitty, as

she was called by her close friends, had been the un-disputed incomparable seven years ago, at the time of Olivia's short-lived come-out.

"I believe we met some years ago. You are Miss Windham, are you not?"

"I was. Now I am Lady Selby. And you were?"

Warmth invaded Olivia's cheeks. "I was, and still am, Olivia Mallory, of Suffolk."

"Yes, of course. I remember now. You were called home early in the season. A family bereavement, I believe."

"My parents. *Our* parents, actually," Olivia said, in-dicating Esme, who had stepped back to give the lady some breathing room. "Lady Selby, may I present my sister, Miss Esme Mallory?"

Esme dropped a curtsy, then bent to reclaim the silk parasol. While she was still on a dog's eye level, she heard footsteps approaching at a fast pace and turned in time to see a pair of well-polished military boots stop very near her.

"Here is my brother," Lady Selby said, "at last."

Her color was rapidly returning, and with it her spir-its. "Joel, you will be happy to know that I am much better now, a circumstance that is due entirely to the kindness of these two nice young ladies, who came to my rescue. Pray, be a dear and help me to thank them."

The gentleman let out a sigh of relief. "Thank them? Nothing so paltry, Kitty, for I mean to throw myself at their feet in undying gratitude. It must be obvious to even the meanest intellect that I am no good whatever when a female feels unwell."

"Gentlemen seldom are at their best in such times," Olivia replied. "Though I must say a pair of strong arms can come in quite handy if the female needs to be carried someplace."

"There you have it then," he said, "we cowardly sorts have our uses."

"Forgive me, Lieutenant, but I cannot permit any-one, not even yourself, to call a man who wears our country's uniform a coward."

The gentleman bowed to Olivia. "I stand cor-rected, ma'am."

Having taken his correction in good part, he reached down a hand to assist Esme to her feet. "Allow me," he said, and once she was her full five feet four inches, she looked directly into the shiny buttons of an infantryman's red tunic. Her breath caught in her throat, for she did not need to look up to know to whom the tunic belonged. Her senses told her the wearer was the gentleman she had seen in Hatchard's the day before, the hero with the black leather eye patch.

"Th-thank you, sir."

"Miss Mallory. Miss Esme. Pray allow me to present my brother, Lieutenant Joel Windham."

Both Olivia and Esme curtsied, and finally Esme looked into the gentleman's face. "The eye patch," she said, noticing that his right eye was no longer cov-ered. "You are not wearing it."

He did not bother asking how she knew about the patch. "I saw the physician only this morning, and he said I might leave it off."

"And your sight? Is it restored?"

"Perfectly," he replied, smiling down at her, "and only just in time."

If the sincerity in his voice was not enough, the look of real admiration in his eyes was sufficient to tell even the most disinterested party that Lieutenant Windham found everything about the lovely young lady to his liking.

As for his sister, her ladyship had regained her health and her composure enough to notice the pretty blonde as well, though the majority of her attention was centered on the older sister. "Forgive my imperti-nence, Miss Mallory, but your hair color is most un-

usual. Would one be safe in calling that particular
shade strawberry blond?"

"You may call it whatever you choose, Lady Selby.
Because the color has long been the bane of my existence, there is little I have *not* called it. My torment,
my affliction, my cross to bear; these are but a few of
the epithets I employ on a regular basis."

Kitty smiled, pleased to discover that her new acquaintance was without an excess of vanity. Quite certain that one at least of her older acquaintances had
referred to the color as blond with just a touch of red,
she remarked that she found the shade quite charming. "But I will not put you to the blush, Miss Mallory.
Instead, may I offer you and your sister a seat in my
landau? Unless, of course, you came in your own
carriage."

"As a matter of fact, we sent our traveling coach
back to Suffolk the day we arrived, and we would very
much appreciate a seat in your carriage. That is, if
Grillon's Hotel is not too far out of your way."

"Grillon's, you say?" Kitty smiled again, pleased to
have the last of the clues fall into place. "I wonder,
Miss Mallory, do you and Miss Esme have plans for
the evening?"

"Please say you do not," her brother added, causing
roses to bloom in Miss Esme's cheeks.

Esme looked to her sister for guidance, and for just
an instant thoughts of Cousin Jane's diary flashed
through Olivia's mind. Such thoughts were quickly discarded, however, for even if she had not been witness
to the hopeful look in Esme's eyes, she would have
chosen any alternative to invading her cousin's privacy. "Our plans are not fixed, Lady Selby. At least
not so much so that they could not be altered to fit
some other evening."

Her ladyship's smile was every bit as winning as
Olivia remembered. "Wonderful," the lady said. "I
know my husband will wish to express his appreciation

for your kindness to me, and since he has a box on Wednesdays at Covent Garden, what could be better than for you and Miss Esme, and anyone else in your party, to join us in our box."

"An excellent notion," the lieutenant said. "Are you fond of the theater, Miss Esme?"

"I cannot say," she replied, "for I have never been. But I am persuaded I shall love it of all things."

"As do I," echoed the military gentleman, who less than an hour ago had informed his sister, in no uncertain terms, that he would rather take a bullet in the arm than be forced to sit through one of those demned boring historical plays.

Lady Selby, unable to ignore the interest her brother was showing in the younger Miss Mallory, chose not to remind him of his previous evaluation of Mr. Shakespeare's works. There were times when too good a memory was not a desirable trait in an older sister. "It is all settled then," she said. "We shall stop by Grillon's at half past seven. If that is agreeable to you."

"Perfectly agreeable," Olivia replied. "Your ladyship is very kind."

"Not at all. And, please, call me Kitty, for I mean to call you Olivia, if I may. I have a feeling that we are destined to be friends."

It had been seven years since Olivia had seen a play. And thanks to their uncle's puritanical strictures, Esme had never set so much as a foot inside a theater. For those reasons alone, it was not to be wondered at that both young ladies were practically giddy with excitement about the coming evening.

Added to the anticipated pleasure of the play was the unqualified distinction of being the guests of Lord and Lady Selby. Olivia recalled dancing with Lord Selby on one occasion during her brief come-out, and at that time he was considered quite a matrimonial prize. Now, she could well imagine that he and his charming wife were among the crème de la crème of the *ton*.

As for her ladyship's handsome brother, though Esme said not a word on the subject of his being one of the party, her silence told its own story. Clearly, his attendance guaranteed that what promised to be a wonderful evening would, instead, be a perfect one.

"Lord luv us," Hepzebah said. After putting the finishing touches on Esme's simple hairstyle, she stepped back to appraise her handiwork. "There'll be none to match you, Miss Esme. Such a picture as you make in that lavender georgette."

The dinner dress was simply cut, as suited a young lady of nineteen summers, with two rows of gossamer puffs at the hem and a mauve velvet ribbon circling beneath the bosom. The maid had threaded a second mauve ribbon through Esme's blond tresses, and the effect was unpretentious, yet enchanting.

Olivia, had she but known it, was every bit as appealing as her younger sister. Her gown was a square-necked, *crème maline* draped over an indigo blue silk underdress, and she did not need the looking glass to tell her that the blue of the silk lent a hint of its color to her gray eyes. Content with what she saw, she completed the ensemble with a double strand of pearls that had once belonged to her mother.

"Oh, Livvy," Esme said, admiration in her voice, "you look beautiful. Mother would be so proud."

The mention of their mother was nearly Olivia's undoing, for dressing for an evening of gaiety had brought back sad, yet sweet memories of her last days with her parents. After swallowing a lump that attempted to lodge in her throat, she thanked Esme for the compliment. "If nothing else, my dear, I daresay we shall not embarrass our host and hostess."

It was not to be wondered at that Lieutenant Windham's appraisal was much warmer than Olivia's. As the party alit from the Selbys' landau and passed beneath the Grecian Doric portico at the Bow Street entrance, the military gentleman whispered to his brother-in-law that unless he missed his guess, the entire theater would soon be abuzz over the beauty of the ladies adorning the Selby box.

"Right you are," Tristan replied. "A blonde, a brunette, and a redhead. And all three as pretty as they can stare."

Joel Windham smiled. "We are a pair of lucky dogs."

Because his lordship was of a similar opinion, he was not surprised when, during the first intermission, several young bucks he barely nodded to at his club found excuses to present themselves at his box. The invasion was repeated at the second intermission, but by this time Tristan Selby had grown annoyed by the interruptions. "Demned nuisances," he whispered to his young brother-in-law, whose handsome countenance had begun to resemble that of a decidedly belligerent watchdog.

As for the ladies, they were enjoying themselves immensely. In the years to come, neither of the Misses Mallory would be able to describe so much as a single scene from *Richard III*, but they would remember perfectly the many flattering compliments paid them by the myriad of young men who came to shake Lord Selby's or Joel Windham's hand.

At first, Esme had been on the edge of her chair, fascinated by the noisy groundlings who paraded back and forth in the pit, calling to one another and ogling any pretty female who happened past. Later she allowed Lieutenant Windham to call her attention to the elegant boxes, which were separated by slender, richly gilded pillars. Within the boxes, the beautifully dressed patrons exhibited at least a degree more decorum than the groundlings.

Not that Esme was the only one fascinated by her

fellow theatergoers. Olivia noticed that Kitty Selby often ignored the action on the stage, choosing instead to peruse the other boxes for a glimpse of people she knew. At one point, with her opera glasses raised to her eyes she paused, then chuckled. When Olivia looked toward the box Kitty was observing, she saw that it was occupied by two people, a matron in her mid-forties and a gentleman who also held opera glasses to his eyes.

Unless Olivia was much mistaken, the gentleman was looking directly at Kitty, and he was chuckling as well.

At the final intermission, there was a rap at the door to their box. "Botheration!" Lord Selby said. "Are we to have no peace the entire evening?"

The question was obviously rhetorical, for Kitty called permission to enter. When the door was opened, the matron from the box across the way stood with her hand on the arm of the man with the opera glasses.

"Kitty, my dear," said the matron's escort, "what a surprise. Did you tell me you were coming to the theater?" Unless Olivia missed her guess, the gentleman's deep, pleasant voice was tinged with suppressed laughter, as was Kitty's when she replied.

"Must I tell you all my plans, my lord?"

"Tell me only that you will forgive this intrusion. Aunt Augusta and I are not staying for the farce, and she wished to speak to you before we left."

Lord Selby and Lieutenant Windham had stood at the couple's entrance, partially obscuring Olivia's view. Even so, though she could not see him, and had never before heard him speak, she knew immediately that the gentleman was the same man she had seen in Grillon's lobby.

"Mrs. Crighton," Kitty said, "how nice of you to stop by. It is always a pleasure to see you, ma'am. You do not, I believe, know our new friends, the Mallorys, who are just arrived from Suffolk for a short stay in town." She took Olivia's hand, obliging her to stand, and presented her to Mrs. Augusta Crighton. "Pray allow me to present Miss Olivia Mallory and her sister, Miss Esme Mallory."

The sisters curtsied and exchanged pleasantries with Mrs. Crighton; then, almost as an afterthought, Kitty made them known to the lady's nephew. "Oh, and this is our old and very dear friend, Lord Crighton."

"Charmed," he said, bowing first to Olivia, then to Esme.

The other gentlemen had finally stepped aside, allowing the sisters a full view of the newcomer, and after Esme's gasp of surprise, followed by a slight stammer, she gained control of her emotions enough to say all that was proper. As for Olivia, she seemed to have lost the ability to speak in coherent sentences. She babbled something that passed for a civility, then fell silent, content to stare at the man who had not been far from her thoughts for the past three days.

He was even larger than she remembered, at least an inch over six feet tall, and he was also broader in the shoulders. His beautifully cut mulberry-colored evening coat, though not as ridiculously snug as those worn by many gentlemen of the *ton*, could not hide his powerful physique—a physique whose hardness apparently rivaled that of a stone wall. In addition to appearing far more fit than the typical London gentleman, it was obvious from the golden tan of his complexion and the slight roughness of his hands that David Crighton spent the majority of his time at something other than evening parties and card tables.

When Olivia had seen him before, in Grillon's lobby, she had thought him more compelling than handsome. Now, as he smiled down at her, causing a noticeable weakness in her knees, she decided that for a man as dangerous-looking as David Crighton, the last thing in the world he needed was to be handsome.

His chin was carved rather harshly, and his nose, which might once have been unremarkable, gave some indication of having come into contact with an angry fist, then allowed to mend without the benefit of medical assistance. Not that either of those features remained long in Olivia's mind, not once she gazed into those mesmerizing, dark blue eyes.

"I believe, Miss Mallory, that I saw you the day you and your sister arrived in town."

Embarrassed by the fact that one look from him had caused a cacophonous pounding behind her temples, Olivia was tempted to deny having seen him. Fortunately, she thought better of it in time to stay the words. He knew she had seen him. He could not help but know it, and to deny it now would only make her look a complete ninnyhammer. "You may have seen us," she said, striving for something resembling an air of nonchalance.

There was a slight pull at the corners of his mouth; not a full smile, but enough to let her know that she had been wise not to deny what had passed between them. "As well," he continued, "I believe I heard you ask the concierge about the possible locations of some poetry societies. Had he any suggestions to offer?"

She shook her head. "Not any that proved really useful."

"In that case, perhaps I might be of service to you, for I—"

His lordship's very surprising offer was cut short by the appearance of the theater's bell ringer, who began pushing his way through the crowd of rowdy groundlings, ringing the large hand bell he carried and announcing the end of the intermission and the beginning of the farce. Because there was always a possibility that the occupants of the box might be interested in what was happening on the stage, good manners decreed that visitors not stay beyond the bell.

For this reason, Lord Crighton and his aunt made rather hasty farewells and took their leave.

The door had only just closed behind them when Kitty Selby leaned forward and whispered into Olivia's ear. "My, my," she said. "What a surprise that you and Lord Crighton had already met. It is a small world, is it not?"

Chapter Five

*N*ever having traveled, Olivia had no way of knowing if the world was or was not a small place. By the afternoon of the following day, however, she had decided the sitting room of their hotel suite was not big enough to contain her and her moonstruck sister. Especially not when the weather had turned against them.

The entire day had been as inclement as any Olivia had ever seen, with water falling from the sky in one never-ending sheet and thunder rumbling loudly enough to rattle every window in the suite. Conversation was impossible, though Esme was heard to bemoan more than once that the rain made it impossible for anyone to venture out-of-doors. After sighing, she said, "Surely even the heartiest of individuals would be hard pressed to call on such a day as this."

"Oh," Olivia replied, her tone unforgivably sarcastic, "were you expecting someone?"

Esme's cheeks turned a bright pink, though Olivia was quite certain the color had nothing to do with the fact that her sister occupied one of the blue brocade wing chairs that flanked a very cozy fire.

"I beg you," Esme said, "do not make sport of me. Not today."

Feeling guilty for having teased the nineteen-year-old, who had apparently earned herself her very first beau, Olivia set aside the petit point she had not actually touched for the past half hour and begged Esme's pardon. "I am a poor excuse for a sister."

"No, no. You are the kindest and best of—"

"Furthermore," Olivia added, motioning toward the half-dozen lace-wrapped pink roses Esme held in her hand, "when a young lady receives a nosegay as lovely as that, it is only to be expected that she would be wishful of seeing the sender. Naturally, you will want to thank Lieutenant Windham for his thoughtfulness."

All embarrassment gone, the young lady beamed. "It was thoughtful of him, was it not?"

"Unquestionably."

Esme fetched from her pocket the small white pasteboard card that had accompanied the roses, and though after six readings Olivia knew the words by heart, her sister read them aloud once again. "Welcome to London. May the memory of your stay be one you will always treasure."

Following another sigh, Esme said, "Not that I think his sending the nosegay was anything more than common politeness."

Olivia did not bother to point out that the military gentleman's politeness had not prompted him to send *two* nosegays. After all, both sisters were visiting London. Still, she did not want to say too much and raise false hopes in her sister's breast, not when Lieutenant Windham was still an officer in the infantry and she and Esme would be returning to Suffolk in less than a fortnight. Lieutenant the Honorable Joel Windham, though the viscount's youngest son, was still a most desirable *parti*, and if he was truly interested in Esme, and she in him, they would work the logistics out between them without any need of outside assistance.

Olivia sincerely hoped that Esme would find love and happiness, but she wanted that love to unfold naturally, without interference or meddling from outside parties—older sisters included. For some reason, and

it was one she had never understood, people always
seemed to think they knew exactly what the young
should do, especially what young females should do.
Their elders could make the most horrendous mess of
their own lives, and be living in never-ending misery,
yet still believe themselves fit to guide others.

It was the worse sort of conceit to believe that
greater age, or kinship, or more education made one
wise enough to know what others should do to insure
their happiness and well-being. And as in Uncle Raeford's case, it was the most unforgivable sort of bul-
lying to imply that one person owed it to another to
heed unsolicited advice.

Olivia wanted none of that for herself or her sister.
Let Esme make her own choices; after all, if she made
mistakes—and she would do so—she would be the one
to live with them. Surely nothing could be less condu-
cive to a young girl's future happiness than other people attempting to tell her what she should think and
how she should feel.

Olivia was to remember that thought half an hour
later when Esme went to the window for the fiftieth
time, sighed for the hundredth time, then returned to
the fire. "I . . . I suppose I could write the lieutenant
a note, thanking him for his thoughtfulness."

*Or you could sit down and stop making a cake of
yourself!* Olivia's patience was obviously at an end,
and afraid she might gave voice to words she would
later regret, she excused herself and went to her
bedchamber.

In truth, she had procrastinated long enough about
opening Jane's diary, and it was time she got busy.
Besides, the thought of another hour of Esme's sighs
lent a certain palatability to what had previously figured as an onerous task.

Of course, if Olivia were truly honest, she would
admit that her sister's behavior might not have seemed
nearly so annoying if *she*, too, had received a floral

tribute. Not from Lieutenant Windham, of course, but from some other gentleman.

Some other gentleman? "You are such a coward!" she said to the face in her looking glass. "Why not say Lord Crighton and be done with it, for that is who you mean. A tribute from any other gentleman would be just so many posies. A polite gesture, nothing more."

She made a face at her reflection. "And you are also an imbecile, Olivia Mallory, for entertaining even the smallest hope that his lordship would send some indication that he meant to further the acquaintance."

Though Olivia had spent a goodly portion of the night before staring at the darkened ceiling of her bedchamber, recalling David Crighton's suggestion that he might be of service to her, by dawn she had convinced herself that he had said it merely to be civil. It was the way of the *ton* to make polite comments they did not actually mean. "How nice of you to come," a hostess might say when, in fact, she thought the guest a dead bore and wished he had gone elsewhere.

Of course, Lord Crighton need not have said anything if he did not mean it. But he had, and— "Desist!" she told the woman in the looking glass. "You are beginning to sound like Esme, and what is forgivable in a moonstruck girl of nineteen is foolish beyond permission in a woman of five and twenty!"

Determined to think of David Crighton no longer, Olivia sat down at the little cherry Davenport desk, slid back the green leather-covered top, and removed Jane's diary. Beside it lay the small key Jane had worn on a gold chain around her neck. After taking a deep breath, then letting it out slowly, Olivia carefully inserted the key in the lock. A mere half turn was needed before the clasp popped open, and there before her lay all her cousin's secrets—secrets Jane had never meant to share with another soul.

Feeling like a betrayer, Olivia forced herself to read the first entry.

> *I have a friend. A poet. I wrote to him merely to tell him that I admired a sonnet of his that I read in "The Poet's Journal." The periodical was several years old, and I was not certain the publisher would forward my letter. I certainly never expected a reply. Not from a writer so famous and so gifted.*
>
> *I tremble each time I reread his letter, for in it he says that he feels our minds are in sympathy, and that it was fate that led me to read that old "Poet's Journal."*
>
> *He asked if he might read one of my poems, and now I am in a quake as to which I should choose.*
>
> *I am six and thirty, a spinster of no particular charm or beauty, and as such I am practically invisible to all who know me. And yet, a famous poet believes us to be simpatico. A man whose words are pure magic wishes to know more of me and my poetry.*
>
> *I have a friend. I, who have been so lonely for such a very long time.*

Olivia set the diary aside; then, with her elbows propped upon the green leather of the desktop, she hid her face in her hands. This was even more difficult than she had imagined it would be. Guilt assailed her, for she had never asked herself if Cousin Jane was lonely. With the carelessness of youth, she had accepted the care and kindness Jane had given her, much as she accepted the loyal service of Hepzebah Potter.

The difference was that Hepzebah was an employee, one who received a monetary reward for her time and attention. Jane Frant had loved two motherless girls without reservation, and not once had either of those girls considered the possibility that their cousin might be lonely, and in need of a friend.

Olivia remained quiet for some time, wishing it were not too late to show Jane how much she was loved and appreciated. Unfortunately, wishing served no purpose, and when the storm outside picked up force and numerous raindrops fell down the chimney to splatter and sizzle against the hot, cast-iron fender, Olivia forced herself to return to her cousin's diary. Several weeks' worth of entries were made before the poet was mentioned again.

> *I am indebted to Mrs. Blair for her willingness to accept any correspondence bearing my name. Because of her, I have another letter from my friend. He admires my poem and begs to see more.*
>
> *I have never been so happy.*

So, the village seamstress was the means by which Jane had received her letters. Olivia had wondered how her cousin had managed to keep her correspondence a secret from Uncle Raeford, who would have disapproved.

Actually, disapproved was too mild an expression. Raeford Frant would have felt betrayed, and to repair the damage done by what he considered familial disloyalty, he would have insisted that his daughter pray for guidance in the matter. Since even heavenly guidance was augmented by words of strictest instruction from Raeford himself, Jane had been wise to keep this part of her life a secret from her father.

Olivia continued to read, though the next dozen or so pages contained nothing but the minutia of Jane's quiet, uneventful life. Finally there was another reference to her friend.

*A packet from "D" today. Enclosed was an-
other letter, plus more of his wonderful poetry.*

*What joy it is to be admired by one who is
truly admirable. His poems are the warm gold of
the sun. The icy blue of a mountain stream. The
crisp whiteness of new-fallen snow. They are all
this and more, and still he admires my poor
efforts.*

My heart is very full. Is this . . . can it be love?

Olivia closed the diary. She had read enough for
one day. More than enough. An old adage warned
that eavesdroppers never heard good of themselves,
but no one had ever warned her that a person who
reads another's secrets may find herself sharing in that
other person's pain.

Sadness weighed upon her heart. And to what end?
It was too late to comfort her cousin, and Olivia had
gained little in the way of clues to the poet's identity.

Mrs. Blair might have remembered the name on
the letters she had received and saved for Jane Frant;
unfortunately, the seamstress was on holiday with her
sister somewhere in Leeds, so Olivia could not write
to her.

The man's name began with a "D." But was that
his given name or his surname? It was such a trivial
piece of information, and Olivia had to wonder if even
an important clue was worth betraying Jane's trust—
a trust that her most private thoughts would remain
so, even after her death?

Olivia had no answer to her question, and she was
more than happy when Hepzebah scratched at the
bedchamber door and interrupted such unproductive
thinking. "The tea tray's here, Miss Livvy, and besides
some little sandwiches, there are jam tarts. If you've
a mind to have one, you'd best come right away, for
you know Miss Esme and her sweet tooth."

For all Olivia cared, Esme could devour every last sweet in the hotel, but she seized the excuse to lock the diary and put it, along with the key, back inside the Davenport desk. After sliding home the green leather cover, Olivia stood, allowing herself a few moments to calm her emotions before rejoining her sister.

When she returned to the sitting room, Esme's sighs had given way to a broad smile. "Sit here," she said, patting the place beside her on the rose velvet settee. "I have poured you a cup of tea, and should you wish to sweeten the Bohea, you will notice a little surprise lying beneath the sugar tongs."

"A surprise? What sort of—"

"Here," Esme said. Obviously unable to wait, she grabbed up the sealed letter that lay beneath the tongs and waved it about like a flag. The missive bore no stamp indicating its place of origin, so Olivia assumed it had been hand delivered.

"It is for you, Livvy. Read it, do, before I positively expire of curiosity."

Because her name was written in a decidedly masculine scrawl, Olivia was tempted to take the missive to her bedchamber where she might read it in private. Two things kept her where she was: her sister's excitement and the nagging suspicion that by reading Jane's diary she had somehow forfeited her own right to undisputed privacy.

Breaking the neat, gold-edged wafer that sealed the missive, she opened the single sheet of white vellum. "It is from Lord Crighton."

Esme squealed with delight. "I knew it must be. Quickly, what does he say?"

Olivia read through the two short paragraphs; then, hoping the warmth in her cheeks did not give her away, she folded the missive in quarters and slipped it inside her sleeve. "He asks if he might show me Hyde Park," she said as calmly as possible.

"When? Surely not today, for the weather is—"

"Esme, do not be a goose. The invitation is for tomorrow. Sometime around four."

Only later, when in the privacy of her bedchamber, did Olivia remove the sheet of vellum from her sleeve and read through it once again. And as before, her cheeks grew warm.

Miss Mallory,

Pray allow me the pleasure of driving you to Hyde Park tomorrow afternoon, weather permitting.

Since the first moment I saw you, I have wanted to know you better . . . your thoughts, your dreams, your past, your present. If you have an ounce of compassion in your heart, you will be waiting at four of the clock.

And will you be so good as to wear a hat with a turned back brim, for it is my wish to spend the entire drive studying your very beautiful face.

Until tomorrow, I am
Yr. Obt. Serv.
Crighton

Chapter Six

At four of the clock the next day, Olivia stood beside the fireplace in the sitting room, her senses attuned to every sound in the corridor outside their suite. Her emotions were in a turmoil. She had never been so excited in her life, for just the thought of spending time with Lord Crighton was enough to make her heart race at a startling speed; especially since he had already expressed his wish to know her better.

And yet, the last seven years weighed on her more than she would have thought possible, and somewhere in the recesses of her mind, a voice that sounded very like Uncle Raeford's warned her against becoming involved with a man of mystery. Who was he? the voice asked. And more importantly, why had he singled Olivia out for his attentions?

She had dressed appropriately for an airing in the park, having chosen to wear a yellow challis walking dress with a gold velvet spencer and a petit point reticule. Because of the contents of his lordship's invitation—or perhaps in spite of it—she had selected a chip straw bonnet whose brim covered half her face, and whose silk veil obscured those areas the brim missed.

The small ormolu clock on the mantel had begun to chime, and just as it sounded the hour, there was a knock at the door. Suddenly unsure of herself and her attire, Olivia waited nervously, her fingers laced to keep them from trembling, while Hepzebah opened the door.

Lord Crighton, upon being admitted to the suite, took one look at Olivia and burst out laughing. "Nice hat," he said by way of greeting.

The man had the manners of a Philistine!

Esme and Hepzebah exchanged questioning looks, but Olivia chose to show no reaction whatsoever. If she hoped that would be the end of it, however, she had much to learn about David Crighton. After exchanging the barest of civilities with Esme, he took Olivia's arm and led her from the suite. The moment they were in the hotel corridor, out of hearing of her sister and the servant, he turned Olivia so she was obliged to look at him. "Coward," he said.

"I am sure I do not know what you mean, my lord."

"You know," he said. "And I warn you, if you mean to turn missish on me, I shall have no recourse but to claim some sort of compensation from you."

Momentarily taken aback, she said, "You would exact a penalty?"

"I believe the word I used was 'compensation.' "

"Are they not one and the same?"

He leaned so close his warm breath teased the lobe of her ear and caused a deliciously prickly sensation all along the nape of her neck. "Not the way I kiss."

The remark was so outrageous Olivia could not help but laugh. "Sir, you are a cad to tease me thus, and if I had even a modicum of sense, I would turn around this instant and rejoin my sister."

"In the first place, madam, I am not teasing. And in the second place, if you had any sense, you would not have worn that hat."

Without asking her permission, he lifted the veil from her face and tossed the transparent silk over the back of her bonnet. "Sir, I never gave you leave to—"

"Shh," he said softly.

Having dispensed with the veil, he took her hand and placed it in the crook of his arm, then led her down the wide, carpeted stairs. "I would not want you to trip, Miss Mallory." Nothing more was said, leaving her to wonder if the remark was meant to explain his taking her arm or his removing her veil.

Outside on Albemarle Street, the sun shone as if it had been ordered especially for those who wished to drive in the park. Clearly Olivia and Lord Crighton were not the only ones desirous of enjoying the lovely weather, for several rather expensive equipages waited at the curb, with footmen or grooms holding the horses' bridles while the drivers were inside the hotel. The smartest of those vehicles was a green and gold curricle pulled by a pair of matched chestnuts, and for some reason Olivia was not surprised when Lord Crighton handed her up into that very curricle.

"Very handsome," she said, once he had climbed aboard and taken the reins.

"You are quite kind, Miss Mallory. Actually, I do not rate my looks much above passable, but if you think me hand—"

"Sir! I referred to the horses."

"You don't say so. Well, there's a facer!"

Olivia felt her lips twitch, but she schooled them into obedience. "If that is cant, my lord, I will thank you to mind your tongue."

"Ah," he said, "so we are back to discussing kisses."

"Sir! You . . . you are—"

"Adequately compensated for the hat," he said, "so I will tease you no more. In fact, to demonstrate to you just how amenable a fellow I can be, I beg you will choose the topic of conversation. I make no restrictions and set no limitations. Pray, choose whatever will conform to your notion of suitable discourse."

When she said nothing, merely stared past the

horses to the many gentlemen's carriages traveling down Piccadilly toward Park Lane, he introduced the subject of the weather. "How nice to see a bit of sunshine."

"Yes. Very nice."

"Though, it is unseasonably cool for April."

"Yes. Very cool."

"I hope we may see a few flowers in the park."

"Yes. So do I."

"Would you like me to put my arm around you?"

"Yes— I mean, no! I would not."

He chuckled. "I thought not, but with you apparently stuck on 'yeses,' I had nothing to lose by trying for an answer I would like."

Olivia, deciding that two could play this game, said, "If it is a 'yes' answer you want, Lord Crighton, you have only to ask a question I would like to hear."

"Indeed? And what might that be?"

"Oh, I do not know. Perhaps you could . . ."

When she hesitated, he prompted her to continue. "I could what, Miss Mallory?"

Though she was to wonder later what demon had taken possession of her brain, she smiled sweetly at him and said, "Perhaps you could say, 'Miss Mallory, will you marry me?' "

There was a slight intake of breath; otherwise, he showed no reaction.

"As it happens, my lord, I have it on excellent authority—your friend, Kitty Selby, to be specific—that you are a matrimonial prize well worth winning. She also informs me—you being so charming, and suave, and handsome—that once it is known you are in town, every lady with a marriageable daughter will be bombarding you with invitations to balls, card parties, routs, and soirees. For that reason, if you care to avoid the crush and propose marriage right this minute, I shall be most happy to oblige you."

"What I propose," he said, "is that we stop by the

Selbys' town house so that I may throttle that excellent authority you quoted."

It was Olivia's turn to laugh. "So, what is sauce for the goose is not necessarily sauce for the gander. You may tease me, but I may not reciprocate."

When he offered no reply, she bade him forget about stopping by the Selbys' town house. "There is no need, sir, for I have decided to take back my offer to consider your offer."

"Oh? And why is that?"

"Because you mentioned throttling poor Kitty. Now that I see you are given to violence, I find I have lost all desire to marry you."

If she interpreted correctly the look he gave her, throttling *her* had also crossed his mind.

"Since I am no longer in my first blush of youth, there are those who might think me desirous of obtaining a husband by whatever means possible. They would be wrong. I am not at my last prayers, but even if I were, I cannot think I would ever be so desperate as to tie myself to a man given to violence, or one whose sole recommendation is that the matchmaking mamas think him worth the effort to capture. So, my lord, you may breathe easy, for I think I will not have you after all."

"Madam, you have the tongue of a viper."

"Sad but true, my lord. Sadder yet, there are those who account it to be my best quality."

At this he spared a moment from watching the traffic to study her face. "Clearly, anyone who would say that has never looked into your eyes."

The words were spoken quietly, and without a trace of levity, and as Olivia returned his penetrating stare, unable to look away, she felt as though her heart might actually thump its way out of her chest.

"That day I saw you in the hotel lobby," he continued, "it was your eyes that bewitched me. Even at a distance, I knew they were quite the loveliest eyes I

had ever seen. Gray as the Channel when you are
thinking serious thoughts, yet rimmed with a soft sil-
very blue when you smile."

Silenced at last, Olivia marveled at the sudden
breathlessness caused by his quiet remark. Following
close on the heels of that sensation was an unexpected
desire to untie the bonnet she wore and fling it into
the street. Now that she gave the matter some
thought, it might be quite nice to be studied at length
by a man who admired her eyes.

Calling herself a fool for even thinking such
thoughts, she forced her mind in another direction.
Saying the first thing that entered her head, she asked
him how his aunt had liked last evening's play.

Thankfully, he took the hint and allowed her to
change the course of their conversation. "She enjoyed it
prodigiously. And what of you? Was it to your liking?"

"Oh, yes. I have not been to the theater in ages,
and just to see the costumes and to hear the laughter
and the applause was more exciting than I can say.
The farce was wonderful as well. You should have
remained to see it. I laughed so hard I was obliged to
borrow Lord Selby's handkerchief to wipe the tears
from my face."

"And what of the words of Mr. Shakespeare? Considering your appreciation of poetry, I should think
you would find the drama most uplifting."

To David's surprise, his remark caused her to blush.

"Actually, my lord, I am no connoisseur."

"No? From your request to know about poetry societies, I had assumed you to be a budding poet."

She shook her head. "I fear my talent is of the
'roses are red, violets are blue' variety. And even then
I find if difficult to rhyme the third line."

"That bad?"

"Worse, actually."

"How so?"

She put her hand to the side of her mouth, as if to

keep any curious observers from reading her lips. "If I confide a secret to you, will you give me your word that it will not ruin me forever in your estimation?"

"Word of a gentleman," he said. "Now confess."

"Be it on your head then, my lord, when I tell you that though I purchased both cantos of Lord Byron's latest work, I found the first canto such slow going that I have not so far been tempted to begin the second."

"What! A young lady who does not swoon at the very mention of the elegant Byron? Madam, I do not know whether to fling you from the carriage as a heretic or smother you with kisses for your discernment."

"There you go again. Violence and kisses. Lord Crighton, I believe you have a two-track mind."

"Actually, Miss Mallory, I would gladly forgo the first track, if you would agree to indulge me in a sampling of the second track."

"Sir, you are truly incorrigible."

For the next few minutes, David gave his attention to the safe turning of the curricle onto Park Lane, where he took his place among the line of splendid carriages progressing slowly through the park. Once that was accomplished, he returned to the subject of poetry. "Am I to understand then, Miss Mallory, that you are no longer interested in pursuing poetry societies?"

"Actually, my lord, I have done so already. I went around to two establishments, though I gained none of the information I sought. A fact I attribute entirely to the stubbornness of those of your sex."

"We males are, admittedly, a recalcitrant lot. That said, allow me to inform you that I refuse to accept any share of the blame without first being apprised of the crimes to which I am expected to confess."

"Foremost," she said, "I must list the totally unfounded belief you males hold that females are mentally inferior beings."

"Ah ha! Now that, at least, is a crime of which I am not guilty."

Her response was a decided *humph.*

"I beg you will acquit me, ma'am, for though I have met half a dozen men this very day who are addle-pated beyond all hope of reclamation, the only ladies I have encountered have been virtual paragons of reason. All, that is, save one particular bird-wit, who chose to wear a wide-poked bonnet when I specifically asked that she do otherwise."

Obviously electing to ignore the reference, she told him about her visits to Carnaby and Lexington Streets. "The secretary of the society on Carnaby Street had not the least notion that he was being insulting when he referred to the creative works of the entire female population as pathetic little poems. Add to that his condescending manner, and you will understand why I kept wishing I had brought a parasol, so I might beat him over the head with it."

"And you call *me* violent?"

She looked directly at him, and the defiant set of her pretty chin made him long to take her in his arms, so he might sip from her lips a sample of her lively spirit. Unfortunately, now was not the time, and a crowded lane was certainly not the place. "What of the establishment on Lexington?" he asked. "Was the secretary there as equally deserving of a taste of your parasol?"

"The president," she replied, all liveliness gone from her voice. "And though he was far more obliging than the first man, there was something about Sir Arthur I could not like."

"Sir Arthur Hix?"

"Why, yes. Are you acquainted with him?"

"No," David said, careful to keep his tone uncommunicative. "I do not know him personally."

They were both silent for a time, and David was actually relieved when someone riding in Rotten Row called out his name.

"Crighton! Is that you?"

A rather plump older gentleman astride a spirited black gelding waved to David, then galloped his horse across the greensward separating the carriage road from the bridle path. "I beg your pardon in advance," David said beneath his breath, "but I must stop for a moment. The gentleman approaching us was a friend of my father's, and I cannot in good conscience ignore his greeting."

"Of course you cannot. Besides, I should enjoy seeing that magnificent animal up close."

"This time, madam, I am quite certain you refer to the horse."

Her laughter was clear and bell-like, and David decided he had never heard anything he enjoyed more. Before he could tell her so, however, the plump gentleman had reined in the handsome gelding with an expertise that was as surprising as it was admirable.

"Crighton. I vow, I have not clapped eyes on you in months. Not since you returned to Kent to recuperate from the wounds you received at the hands of that deuced French cutthroat. How are they by the way? Since you are here in town, may one assume you are on the mend?"

"Sir," David said when he could get a word in, "allow me to make you known to my friend. Miss Mallory, this is one of my neighbors, Mr. George Rice."

The gentleman touched his finger to the curled brim of his beaver hat. "Servant, ma'am."

"How do you do?" the lady said.

"Knew a Mallory once," his neighbor continued. "Sir Inigo Mallory. A military man. Became a general, I believe. Of course, he was not a young man when I knew him, so a pence will earn you a pound he put his spoon in the wall years ago."

"Yes, sir, he did," Miss Mallory said. "About forty years ago."

George Rice seemed taken aback by her reply. "You knew him, then?"

Not by the slightest lifting of an eyebrow did she reveal her shock at the suggestion that she was old enough to have known someone who died forty years ago. "I knew him only by reputation, sir. He was my grandfather. Unfortunately, he did not live to see the births of his granddaughters."

"I say, Crighton, how's that for a coincidence? The young lady's grandfather a hero in the colonies, and you a hero in France."

To David's relief, a man in a Tilbury called out his displeasure at being obliged to wait behind the curricle.

"Deuced yahoos," Mr. George Rice said. "Got no better manners than to interrupt old friends who wish to exchange a few words. In my day, a gentleman knew how to comport himself in the park." Though he gave the fellow in the Tilbury an angry look, he touched his hat to Miss Mallory, then began backing the handsome black out of the way. "When you return to Kent," he called to David, his jovial nature resurfacing, "stop in at the Hall. Take your mutton with Mrs. Rice and me."

"Thank you, sir. I shall be honored."

While the rider and horse returned across the greensward to Rotten Row, David set the curricle in motion. "So," he said, hoping to avoid questions about himself that he felt certain were dancing around in his lovely companion's brain, "your grandfather was a general. Do tell me about him. And, by the way, George Rice is a fool, so if anything he said is preying on your mind, allow me to assure you that you look far too young to have known a man who passed away forty years ago. How old are you by the way? Twenty-one? Twenty-two?"

"No, no, no," she said, wagging her finger at him, "you do not get off that easily, for I will not be distracted by a bit of inane flattery."

"Inane! Why, madam, I will have you know that I

am reputed to be positively silver-tongued. Known for my compliments from Land's End to John o'Groat's."

"That may well be, my lord, and on some other day I shall be happy to allow you to swagger and boast to your heart's content. Today, however, I want to hear how you happened to be in France, of all places, and how you came to be wounded by a cutthroat. Oh, and like your friend, Mr. Rice, may I offer my sincerest hope that you are on the mend?"

"Thank you, I am fully recovered," he said. "But more than that I am not at liberty to say."

"Not at liberty?" As the significance of the phrase became clear to Olivia, she gasped. "Oh, my word! You are a spy. Or at least you were."

He muttered something about having acted as a liaison once or twice, nothing more, but he might as well have saved his breath. Olivia knew when a person was merely toying with semantics.

She had little knowledge of spies, except that they were reputed to be clever and resilient, and not afraid to accept dangerous assignments behind enemy lines. The image fit, for from the first moment she saw him, Olivia had known that David Crighton was no ordinary man; not a man who took the safe route.

Recalling that she had also thought him the type who ate naive country girls for breakfast, she felt a shiver run up her spine. What was she doing with such a man? And more to the point, why was he with her? What were his intentions? From the informality of his manners, she could well imagine that he wished to set up a flirtation with her. But did he hope for more? For something clandestine?

Before she had time to ponder this last and most disturbing question, the sun disappeared and thunder rolled in the distance. Within a matter of moments, carriages were being turned and horses given the office to hurry along home. Hyde Park was a place for beautiful ladies and equally fine-looking gentlemen to

greet friends, to see and be seen, and to show off their
latest finery. Ruining that finery in a sudden downpour
played no part in their plans.

The horses, too, wanted no part of a storm, and
with the first sharp bolt of lightning, Lord Crighton's
chestnuts began to sidestep and pull against the traces.
"Whoa," he called to them. "Steady there, boys. No
reason to become agitated."

With a skill that could not fail to impress, he main-
tained control of the skittish pair and turned the curricle. It was a testament to his competence that he
managed to keep one or two less capable drivers from
running them off the road, and in a surprisingly short
amount of time he halted the chestnuts at the front
entrance of Grillon's Hotel. "I beg you will forgive
me, Miss Mallory, if I do not escort you to the door,
but this pair are far too restive to leave them with
a stranger."

"Think nothing of it," she said, taking the hand he
offered and allowing him to assist her to alight. "I
doubt I shall come to any harm in the five feet from
here to the door. And in the event I am set upon
by thieves and cutthroats while covering that perilous
distance, I daresay there are at least a dozen footmen
ready and willing to come to my rescue."

David Crighton chuckled, then made her a slight
bow.

"You are bravery itself, Miss Mallory."

"Good afternoon, my lord. And thank you for a
pleasant outing."

Any further leave-taking was cut short by a particularly loud clap of thunder. The noise caused the chestnuts to whinny in protest, and the gentleman with the
reins to give his entire attention to keeping the pair
in line.

As for Olivia, she did not relish the idea of becoming a human lightning rod, so she turned and hurried

toward the door, which the uniformed doorman held open for her.

Once inside the lobby, she went to the window that fronted on Albemarle Street and pushed aside the heavy drapery so she could watch Lord Crighton drive away. Large raindrops splashed against the glass, and outside the sky had grown dark as night. As for the curricle and pair, they were gone, and with them the most fascinating man Olivia had ever met.

Not that she had met all that many. Actually, had she been acquainted with a thousand men, it would have made no difference. She knew instinctively that not one of those other men would have engendered in her the sort of excitement she felt when sitting beside David Crighton.

Uncle Raeford would not have approved of the association, and truth to tell, Olivia was not certain she thought it all that wise. David Crighton was a rogue, one who did things his own way, without thought for the danger involved. When she was with him, a bit of his daring seemed to creep into her very soul, making her say and do things that were totally unlike her usual self.

The thing was, she liked the way she felt when in his company. With him she felt free. Uninhibited.

But what of him? How did he feel? He had said he liked her eyes, but was that enough?

"Do you wish to see me again?" she asked beneath her breath.

Naturally, the gentleman did not hear the question, and the raindrops coursing down the window took no interest in the affairs of humans. Olivia was being foolish—she knew that. Even so, something inside her prayed that David Crighton would call upon her again. And soon.

Chapter Seven

On Sunday morning, all three of the visitors from Suffolk attended services at the very impressive Westminster Cathedral, with its majestic twin towers reaching to the heavens. Following the service, Hepzebah joined one of the hotel footmen and his sister for an afternoon in Green Park, apparently having forgotten for the time being the existence of a certain groom back home at Frant House.

Not that the maid was the only one with an unreliable memory. Mr. Vernon Sydney, the worthy neighbor whose proposal of marriage Olivia had promised to consider while in town, did not so much as cross the lady's mind. How could he, when her thoughts were filled with recollections of the time spent with a certain handsome and exciting peer?

After a nuncheon consisting of cold ham and assorted berries in clotted cream, the sisters spent the remainder of the day in quiet pursuits. Though Raeford Frant was no longer there to insure that his nieces gave the day the respect he felt it deserved, they chose not to stray too far from the pattern of behavior established during the last seven years.

By Monday morning, however, Esme was ready to see more of the capital city, and only the sight of the morning post dissuaded her from insisting that they set forth immediately. Propped against the chocolate pot Hepzebah had placed on the table in the sitting room were three letters. One bore Esme's name, while the other two bore Olivia's.

Like a two-edged sword, the missives for Olivia brought welcome tidings and those that were not so welcome.

"Oh, Livvy, look," Esme said, studying the vellum bearing her name, "this one is for me. Shall . . . shall I open it?" she asked, her eyes pleading with her sister to say that it was permissible.

"It is your letter," Olivia said. "I would not dream of reading it first."

"You are the best of sisters!"

After carefully breaking open the wafer, Esme unfolded the single sheet with hands that were not quite steady. "It is from Lieutenant Windham," she said, her voice imbued with an unmistakably dreamy quality.

Olivia noticed her sister's elation, though she chose to pretend otherwise. She was not surprised at the identity of the letter writer, for while Esme was taking such care in opening her very first letter, Olivia had opened and read a handwritten invitation from Kitty Selby. "Lady Selby asks if we will join a small party she is getting up for tomorrow. The destination is to be Richmond."

"I know," Esme said, unable to hide her excitement. "Is it not the most exciting plan? Joel—I mean the lieutenant—says there is to be an alfresco breakfast. Like those you attended when you had your come-out. Oh, Livvy, it is all too, too wonderful!"

Remembering how it had felt to be a young girl, and invited to her first real party, Olivia agreed. "The outing sounds absolutely 'too, too.' As for the breakfast, it is a bona fide pièce de résistance."

"Lieutenant Windham wishes to assure us," Esme said, "that every attention will be paid to our comfort. As well, he says, we need not fear being without sufficient escorts, for he is to be one of the party, along with his brother-in-law, and two gentlemen who are friends of his from his regiment."

Olivia sincerely hoped she was not destined to endure an entire afternoon of "the lieutenant says," when Esme quoted Joel Windham's next words, words that insured her sister's complete attention. "Oh, and the lieutenant says that Lord Crighton has already accepted the invitation."

At this particular piece of information, Olivia's interest in the already interesting invitation went up tenfold. She would see David Crighton again. With her heart singing, she almost missed Esme's next words. "His lordship's uncle and aunt, Mr. and Mrs. Crighton, have been invited as well, but they have not yet replied."

Esme looked up from the letter, her pretty green eyes alight with happiness. "Was it not kind of Lady Selby to invite us? Please say we may go, Livvy. Surely you can have no objections when—"

"I have no objections," she replied, adopting a calmness she did not feel. "No objections at all."

With a squeal of delight, Esme jumped up from the table and threw herself at her sister, hugging her with an enthusiasm that bordered on battery. "Oh, thank you, Livvy. Thank you. You are truly the dearest and best of sisters."

"Miss Esme," Hepzebah said, "unhand Miss Livvy this instant, or you're like to go home to Suffolk without a relative to your name!"

Suitably chastened, Esme begged her sister's pardon, then resumed her seat and poured out cups of chocolate for two. After slathering a piece of toast with marmalade and taking a large bite, she reclaimed her letter and reread it in silence.

Olivia felt a bit of a fraud accepting Esme's gratitude, for declining the invitation had never entered her mind, not when Kitty Selby had been so unbelievably kind to them. And, of course, once Olivia had heard that Lord Crighton was to be one of the party, nothing short of a newly severed limb would have induced her to remain at home.

A footman in Selby livery waited in the corridor for their reply to the invitation, and since both sisters agreed that Esme should pen their acceptance—hers being the legible handwriting—Olivia took a few sips of chocolate, then opened her second letter. The missive was from Sir Arthur Hix.

After a paragraph of flowery commonplaces, the baronet asked if he might call upon Olivia that afternoon.

> You will think me a strange sort of man, but once I get something in my mind, it is all but impossible for me to let it go. I have been thinking about your mystery poet, and the more I ponder the matter, the more I believe I can help you discover his identity.
>
> I quite understand your reluctance to allow your only copies of the poems out of your sight, but I would be more than happy to stop by your suite, if that is agreeable to you, so that I might read the poems there, all at once.
>
> I shall await your reply. Until then, I am
> Yr. Obt. Serv.
> Arthur Hix, Bart.

Olivia set the baronet's letter aside, then wiped her fingers on her napkin. She knew she was being foolish, but for some reason she did not like touching something he had touched. As for the idea of allowing the prissy little man into their suite, just the thought of it gave her the uneasy feeling that Hepzebah liked to call "someone walking over your grave."

Hurrying to her bedchamber, Olivia carefully

penned a note advising the gentleman that her time
was promised both that day and the next. To keep the
baronet from renewing his suggestion of calling upon
her, she told him that she would give herself the pleasure of being in the audience on Thursday afternoon,
when his poetry society welcomed ladies.

What was it about the little man that she could not
like? No, it was more than dislike. Her feelings were
more like revulsion, which was a surprise, for though
there were a few people she did not wish to befriend,
she had never before experienced this sort of aversion.

Whatever it was, she felt certain that Lord Crighton
shared her feelings. Even though he claimed he did
not know Hix personally, there had been a coldness
in his voice when he said it, and that coldness was
enough to tell Olivia that he did not *want* to know
Sir Arthur.

She definitely did not wish to further her acquaintance with the baronet, and though she had no logical
basis for her misgivings, something told her that she
would be wise not to allow him access to the poems.

Not sure where to turn for advice in the matter,
she decided to return to the offices of Quartermaine
Publishing. She had little to report to the publisher,
except for the fact that she had discovered the initial
of her cousin's poet-friend, but she was not above
using that information as her excuse for calling. She
needed information, and if Sir Arthur was a published
poet, chances were Mr. Quartermaine would know
him. If he did, and he had terrible things to say about
the baronet, Olivia would feel perfectly justified in
giving him the cut direct.

Satisfied that she was doing the right thing, she told
Esme she needed to go out for a time. "While I am
gone," she added, to soften the disappointment to her
sister, who had hoped to go to Whitehall for the
eleven o'clock ceremonial mounting of the Horse

Guards, "how would it be if I treated you and Hep-zebah to new hats?"

"Famous!" Esme replied. "I remember seeing a mil-liner's shop several doors down from Hatchard's, on Piccadilly, and in the window was the most adorable villager bonnet. It was framed in grebe feathers and tied with pink ribbons that I am persuaded will per-fectly match the flowers in my new sprigged muslin."

Wisely keeping to herself her opinion of a villager hat trimmed in feathers, grebe or otherwise, Olivia counted from their cash supply four one-pound notes, then gave the money to Esme. "That should be suffi-cient for two of the nicest chapeaux in the shop."

While her sister and the maid went to the small bedchamber to dress for their excursion, Olivia made herself ready to call upon Phineas Quartermaine. Un-sure how long the clement weather would hold, she donned a cloak made of dark blue worsted, trimmed in a lighter blue velvet, then arranged the hood over her hair, securing it with a tortoiseshell hair clip.

When she reached the hotel lobby, she gave a foot-man a half-crown to deliver to Lexington Street the letter she had written to Sir Arthur Hix. "I should prefer that it be delivered to the gentleman himself."

"Not to worry, miss," he said, pocketing the silver coin. "I'll see it's put in the gentleman's own hand."

Happy to have postponed for the moment the meet-ing with Sir Arthur, Olivia allowed the doorman to hand her into a hackney. "Number eleven Holburn," she told the driver.

The ride to the publisher's seemed much shorter than it had the week before, and not surprisingly, this jarvey charged her only one and six, an entire shilling less than the driver from the week before. "I knew it," she muttered, giving the jarvey his fee plus six-pence extra for his honesty.

The morning was a bit blustery, making her glad

she had chosen the warm cloak. Even so, she hurried inside the codestone building, where she gave her name to the same sallow-faced, disinterested clerk. "Mr. Quartermaine said I might call at any time," she said.

The clerk did not even bother to set aside the quill he held. "Up the stairs," he said. "Same as before."

The publisher's door stood open, and he spied Olivia before she reached the top of the stairs. "Good day to you," he said, standing to greet her. "I hope you have come with good news, Miss Mallory, for I am eager to get started on the production of the book featuring your cousin's poems."

"As it happens, Mr. Quartermaine, I have very little to report. Aside from the discovery of a single initial, I am no closer to ascertaining the poet's identity. The major reason I came to see you, sir, is because I have a question or two of my own—questions regarding a gentleman I met at a poetry society."

The publisher took his place behind his desk, and as before, the chair groaned in protest at having to bear his not inconsiderable weight. His face impassive, he said, "The gentleman's name?"

For an instant Olivia hesitated. Now that she was here, her errand seemed somehow distasteful, almost as if she were spying on a person who had done nothing to give her reason to question his sincerity. Nothing at all. And yet, she had learned to trust her instincts, and some inner voice told her that there had to be a reason why she had disliked Sir Arthur almost from the moment she met him.

Taking a deep breath, she put aside her misgivings. "I wonder, Mr. Quartermaine, if you are acquainted with Sir Arthur Hix?"

"The president of that gaggle of would-be poets on Lexington Street?"

"Then you know him, sir?"

"If you are asking have I published his poetry, the

answer is no." The publisher's face was impassive no longer. "The man is a hack, and if paper cost as little as tuppence a ton, I would not waste a sheet of it on the maudlin drivel that comes from his pen."

Well! There was plain speaking indeed.

It appeared the publisher was not finished with his diatribe, for after giving Olivia a measuring look, he continued. "The man's work is uninspired and derivative, his subject matter is trite, and his rhymes are as commonplace as a schoolboy's. And if you've a bee in your bonnet that Sir Arthur is the man who corresponded with your cousin, I will tell you to your face, my girl, that you are wrong."

"No, sir. I thought nothing of the kind."

"Glad to hear it." The publisher settled back in his chair, his emotional outburst seemingly forgotten. "You said you had a question or two, Miss Mallory. What, then, is your second question?"

Olivia told him about visiting Lexington Street, and about Sir Arthur's request to come to Grillon's so he could read the poems. "I do not know why, Mr. Quartermaine, but I am reluctant to be in the man's company."

"Oh, well, as to that, I cannot say I have ever heard anything to darken the fellow's character where the ladies are concerned. I remember hearing once that he had an income from his family's estate, and apparently the sum is sufficient to allow him to indulge himself in his delusion that he is a poet. He published a book of his poems several years ago, at his own expense, but I have never met anyone who actually purchased a copy."

This last was pretty much what Olivia had suspected, and though the information made her even less inclined to trust the baronet with poems her cousin had guarded so carefully, it did not help her find a way to avoid the man.

"You mentioned an initial," the publisher said, as

if to remind her that he had work to do. She told him what she had found, and though he said it was not much to go on, he wrote the "D" on a piece of paper and put it in the top drawer of his desk. "Let me know, dear lady, if you discover anything more."

The large gentleman stood, and Olivia, rightly interpreting this as her dismissal, gathered her cloak around her and descended the stairs.

She exited the building on Holburn Street and stood in the blustery wind, attempting to hail a hackney while assiduously ignoring a man on stilts who walked up and down the street, knocking the hats of unsuspecting pedestrians, then shoving advertising handbills into their coats. At that same time, her sister sat before an oval looking glass in Madame Yvette's Millinery, a pretty shop decorated in muted shades of blue and silver. Olivia's morning may have been unproductive, but Esme had been quite happily employed, trying on one lovely creation after another.

Having made her decision at last, she said, "I vow, madame, your designs are so marvelous that my brain has been in a whirl this hour and more. Even so, I believe I will have the villager with the grebe feathers and the pink ribbons, and that darling little Juliette cap trimmed in the seed pearls."

"Excellent choices, mademoiselle. Though in everything you are *très ravissante.*"

While the thin-faced proprietress hurried to the rear of the shop to find hatboxes of an appropriate size to accommodate the purchases, Esme remained before the looking glass, using the time to try on several more bonnets. She turned first this way then that to get a better view of herself, and as she did so, she happened to make eye contact with a very young lady, one Esme knew had been surreptitiously watching her for the past half hour.

Caught in the act, the young lady blushed, turning her round, childish face the color of a poppy. "The decision must have been difficult," she said. "With your honey-colored hair and green eyes, each hat you tried on was lovelier than the last."

"You are too kind," Esme replied.

"No, no. It is as the proprietress said, you looked quite *ravissante*."

Accustomed to country ways, the nineteen-year-old found nothing to dislike in being addressed by a stranger, especially when that stranger paid her a compliment. Reclaiming the simple straw bonnet she had worn into the shop, Esme tied the ribbons beneath her chin, then turned around, a ready smile on her lips. "Have you found anything you like?"

The young lady, who must have been all of seventeen summers, indicated the dozen or so bonnets stacked on the chair beside her. "I have been here for an hour, and nothing I try looks good on me."

Esme could not help but notice that the stack contained some of the very same hats she had tried on earlier, styles that suited her slender oval-shaped face. Since the girl's face was noticeably round, and still retained a degree of puppy fat, the hats that were becoming to Esme were not at all flattering to her. Furthermore, with her brown hair and brown eyes, it was no wonder the pastel choices did not please her.

Recalling the jewel colors that were so lovely on Lady Selby, Esme said, "I know a lady whose coloring is quite similar to yours, and the other day she wore a jasper green silk that was most becoming."

"Jasper? Oh, but—"

"Just wait. Do not move."

Esme went to the thick oak display shelves that lined the walls, and after searching several shelves and moving aside a number of hats in medium and dark greens, she found a small, brimless silk that was a shade lighter than jasper. "Here," she said, offering the creation to the young lady, "try this."

It was instant perfection. "Oh, my," the young lady

said, tears moistening her eyes, "I had no idea I could . . . could . . ."

"Look so pretty?" Esme finished for her. "It is all a matter of choosing the proper color. Did your mother never tell you that—" She paused, only just realizing that she might be crossing the line of what was pleasing. After all, the girl was a stranger.

"I am an orphan," the young lady said.

"As am I," Esme said. "Fortunately, I have an older sister whose taste is impeccable."

The young lady sighed. "I always wanted a sister. I have an older brother, and though he is everything one could hope for in a brother—kind, brave, and willing to tolerate the company of a silly younger sister—I should still like to have a sister."

She giggled, then spoke in a hushed tone that implied a certain need for confidentiality. "My brother fought in the Peninsula, where he was awarded a medal for bravery, yet when he brought me to this shop, he positively refused to set foot across the threshold. It was almost as if he feared some catastrophe would befall him should he enter such an establishment."

Esme giggled as well. "How very droll. Who would suspect that a gentleman who had faced enemy soldiers would find it so daunting to enter a shop filled with nothing more threatening than ladies' outer garments?"

"Amazing, is it not?"

They shared a laugh at the foibles of gentlemen, then Esme asked if the young lady and her brother resided in London.

"No. We are here only until the first week in June. We have hired a house in Portman Square. My brother insisted that we do so, for he knew it was my mother's wish that I be presented at court, and that I enjoy at least one season in town."

As if only then realizing that Hepzebah was the only other person in the shop, Esme asked the young lady if she had a chaperone.

"Oh, my, yes. James, that is my brother, is a positive martinet about my not going anyplace alone. Usually, Miss Wellesly, my old governess, accompanies me, but today she is laid low with a sick headache. My great-aunt, who is to present me at court, will arrive in town sometime in the next few days, but she insisted that Miss Wellesly be on hand for those less formal occasions when my aunt's presence is not required."

Secretly, Esme hoped the great-aunt had good taste in clothes, and that she meant to help the girl acquire a suitable wardrobe. Especially if the brother wished his sister to make a good impression on the *ton*.

"For now," the young lady continued, "I merely stopped in this shop because my brother had an errand at Manton's shooting gallery, where ladies do not go. He and a friend went to pick up a pistol James had ordered, and they are to come fetch me when they are finished."

Madame Yvette returned with the hatboxes, and while she packed Esme's choices in tissue paper, a dark-haired gentleman in a regimental tunic tapped at the window, then pressed his face to the glass. "There is James now."

Like his sister, the lieutenant was on the short side, and though he was probably twenty-two or -three, he had the same round, youthful face, which he attempted to disguise with a large, bushy mustache.

"Oh," the young lady added, "and there is my brother's friend, Lieutenant Windham."

"Joel?" Immediately Esme pressed her lips shut, embarrassed to have called him by his name.

"Do you know the lieutenant?"

Not wanting to mention the nosegay he had sent her, or the letter that arrived just that morning, she

said, "We were theater guests of his sister, Lady Selby,
the other evening. The lieutenant was one of the
party."

"Famous! Then you do know him. Surely this is the
work of Providence."

Before Esme could determine what the other girl
meant by such a remark, she asked if Esme had any
other engagements that morning. "If not, would you
be so kind as to join us for tea? My brother promised
to take me up the street to Fortnum & Mason's, and
it would be ever so much nicer if another lady came
along. Please say you will, for I have no friends in
town, and I have been so lonely."

When Esme hesitated, the young lady continued.
"Truth to tell, I am not at all clever, and I find it just
a bit overwhelming being in company with two such
impressive soldiers."

Esme wanted to go, but she had never been obliged
to make this sort of decision herself. When she looked
to the back of the shop, where Hepzebah waited for
her, the maid came to her rescue. "I don't think Miss
Livvy would object to your having tea with Lieutenant
Windham and this young lady, who is . . ."

"Oh, forgive me," the girl said, as if only just realizing they had not exchanged names. "I am Agnes Averill, from Upper Corby, in Cambridgeshire."

Hepzebah curtsied. "How do you do, miss? This
young lady is Miss Esme Mallory, from St. Guilford,
Suffolk."

"Suffolk? Why, we are practically neighbors."

The two young people exchanged curtsies, then
after Esme paid for the hats she had selected, and the
one Hepzebah had chosen, she and her new friend
exited the shop.

The smile of welcome on Lieutenant Windham's
face was enough to convince Esme she had made the
right choice. "By Jove!" he said, removing his hat and
making her a sharp, military bow. "The gods must be

in fine fettle today to award me—I mean, *Lieutenant Averill and me*—with such good fortune. I had no idea that you and Miss Averill were friends."

If the statement was not accurate at that moment, it was true enough two hours later, when Miss Agnes Averill, her brother, Lieutenant James Averill, and his old school chum, Joel Windham, escorted Esme from Fortnum and Mason's to Grillon's Hotel. Esme thanked the gentlemen for a lovely tea; then, like two lifelong friends, she and Miss Agnes hugged each other and made plans to meet in two days' time.

"Why not tomorrow?" Joel Windham asked. "Have you been to Richmond, Miss Agnes?"

Agnes looked to her brother, who said they had not yet had an opportunity to take in all the sights. "But if Miss Esme is to go, I know I would never hear the end of it if I said Agnes could not."

"Excellent," Joel said. "I'll go around to my sister's right away and have her send an invitation to Portman Square."

To Esme's delight, the next day was beautiful. The sun shone as though it had mistaken April for July, the sky was cloudless and a perfect blue, and the wind, which had been so blustery the day before, barely ruffled the leaves on the trees. It was, in her words, "A day made in heaven."

Lady Selby sent her landau around to Grillon's to bring Livvy and Esme to her home in Cavendish Square, where the entire party was to meet to decide who drove with whom. At least two of the gentlemen planned to ride, and Lord Selby had graciously offered to provide mounts for the sisters, if they wished to ride.

"I would love to accept his offer," Livvy said. "Unfortunately, since Kitty's interesting condition makes riding inadvisable for her, I feel it behooves me to decline as well."

As for Esme, who was an indifferent rider at the best of times, she had no intention of going anyplace on horseback. "Ten or more miles in the saddle, when I might ride in a well-sprung carriage? I thank you, no."

When they reached Cavendish Square, the Selbys' street was crowded with waiting vehicles and saddle horses reaching all the way to the corner of Wigmore Street. A small band of ladies and gentlemen were gathered around their host, who held a sheet of paper in his hand, and as the Mallory ladies arrived, two fourgons were just pulling away from the curb. The lumbering, utilitarian vehicles were piled high with chairs, tables, food, drink, and enough servants to guarantee that the bucolic outing would be an unqualified success.

While Lord Selby called for quiet, so he could read names off the list provided to him by his wife, Esme and Livvy walked over to an outdated black and gold barouche and shook hands with Mrs. Augusta Crighton, who introduced them to her husband, Mr. Denholm Crighton.

Esme curtsied and Livvy extended her hand. "A pleasure to meet you, sir."

"The pleasure is mine," the gentleman said, though with a noticeable lack of enthusiasm. He had the saddest eyes Esme had ever seen, and once the introductions were completed, he leaned back against the squabs on the hooded side of the carriage, almost as if he wished to hide from view.

His wife, obviously hoping to disguise his discourteous behavior, mumbled something about the weather being felicitous. Livvy replied with some sort of innocuous observation of her own, then she said she thought they had better return to Lord Selby, in case he had already called their names from his list.

Esme was more than willing to return to the noisy group gathered around his lordship, for Joel and

James, plus another military gentleman she did not know, were making everyone laugh with their good-natured insults.

"Poor Mrs. Crighton," Livvy said. "She seemed rather ill at ease."

"And no wonder, with that husband of hers. If he had no wish to be sociable, one wonders why he chose to come."

"Shh," Livvy warned. "He might hear you." She said no more, for Lord Selby had just called her name. "I am here," she said.

"Miss Mallory, you will begin the journey with Lord Crighton, in his curricle."

Though Esme was almost certain that riding with Lord Crighton was exactly what her sister wanted to do, Olivia merely nodded, then turned to compliment Lady Selby on her organizational skills. "You amaze me, Kitty."

"Not at all," her ladyship replied. "One of the benefits of being in my condition is that I am not expected to do anything that would sap my strength. For that reason, I left the entire handling of the food and the servants to the butler."

"And the travel arrangements for your guests?" Livvy asked.

"I merely wrote out the list, my dear Olivia, after heeding a rather broad hint from someone who shall remain nameless."

Who that nameless person might be, Esme could not even guess, and if Livvy knew, she meant to keep the information to herself. In fact, as calmly as if she were paired with the roguish Lord Crighton every day of her life, she opened the green and white striped parasol that matched her green and white taffeta walking dress, then made her way to Lord Crighton's curricle, where a groom helped her to climb up beside the handsome driver, who held the reins to a pair of equally handsome chestnuts.

If the truth be known, Olivia's calm was a facade, for inwardly she was as nervous as a young miss still in the schoolroom. Somehow, she had known she would be paired with David Crighton, and though she was delighted at the prospect of spending an hour or more in his company, she did not want any of the other guests speculating as to the degree of pleasure it gave her.

"You have brought a parasol," David said, giving her a smile so wicked it was guaranteed to warm the heart of any female between the ages of ten and one hundred. "Recalling your propensity for violence, Miss Mallory, should I be on my guard?"

"I should think not, my lord. Not unless you mean to make condescending remarks about the members of my sex."

"Me? Never. I love the ladies too much."

That Olivia could well believe!

He lowered his voice, so only she could hear. "I am especially fond of the ones who are obliging enough to wear hats with turned-back brims."

Olivia felt the heat of embarrassment spread from her face all the way down to her toes. She had not chosen the hat for his lordship's benefit—at least, that was what she had told herself a dozen times or more before she left the hotel. It just so happened that of the hats she had brought to town, the pale green silk suited her ensemble best.

"Miss Esme," Olivia heard Lord Selby say, once he ceased laughing over something outrageous one of the younger gentlemen had said, "you will accompany my brother-in-law in his cabriolet."

"I protest!" Lieutenant Averill shouted. "This is nepotism at its foulest!"

"And Miss Averill," Tristan said, bowing politely to the rather plain young lady, "Lady Selby and I would be pleased if you would join us in the landau."

"Oh, how nice," Kitty said, for all the world as if

it had not been her idea to take the girl in her carriage. "This will give us a chance to become better acquainted."

Agnes Averill looked up at the dashing Kitty with something akin to hero worship. "I should like that of all things, my lady."

"Lieutenant Averill," Tristan Selby said, "you and your friend, Captain Brougthern, will begin the journey on horseback, but in an hour, when we stop to stretch our limbs, you may wish to exchange places with Crighton and my brother-in-law." He chuckled, getting into the spirit of their teasing. "Can't let those two knaves have the single ladies all to themselves."

"Right you are," Lieutenant Averill said, giving his mustache a dramatic twirl. "And if the blackguards refuse to surrender their places, I say we call them out, eh, Brougthern? Pistols at dawn, on Primrose Hill."

The captain, by far the handsomer of the two uniformed riders, said that he would be more than happy to shoot Joel Windham. "Do the world a favor," he added.

Everyone laughed, and within a matter of minutes the grooms stepped away from the various horses' heads and the caravan began the trip to Richmond.

Chapter Eight

*D*avid Crighton could not remember the last time he had wanted to kiss someone as badly as he wanted to kiss Olivia Mallory. Right now, with at least nine people in sight, one of them the lady's sister, all he could think about was reining in the chestnuts, tossing aside that blasted parasol, and taking the gray-eyed enchantress in his arms.

"You are very quiet, my lord."

"Am I?"

"You know you are. Have you something on your mind?"

"As a matter of fact," he said, letting his gaze linger for several moments on her full, tempting lips, "I have."

"Would you care to share?"

Because that was exactly what he wanted, to share a long, soul-searching kiss with her, he laughed. "I should dearly love to share something with you, madam."

"If you can laugh, sir, I am persuaded the matter cannot be too serious."

"As to that, Miss Mallory, I take very few things seriously."

"Not even yourself?"

"Especially not myself."

He said nothing more for perhaps half a mile; then,

though he had not meant to do so, he found himself confiding in her the thoughts that had been in his mind ever since Joel Windham's friends had joked about doing away with each other. "I take life very seriously, Miss Mallory, for I have seen too many deaths to view the gift of life lightly. We humans are far too eager to spill each other's blood."

"Even in jest," she said, obviously connecting his conversation with the scene that prompted it.

"Even in jest," he replied. "Believe me, there is nothing remotely amusing about the taking of a human life. And if there is anything noble in it, in battle or otherwise, I have never seen the evidence."

"But, sir, what if one is in the right?"

"I collect that you mean, 'What if God is on one's side?' "

"For want of a better phrase."

He shook his head, "Madam, that is the most insidious of all phrases! Empty rhetoric spouted by men with political ambition to delude the unwary."

"But—"

"How easy it would be to credit all the misery and devastation of the past years to Napoleon and the people of France when, in truth, we must all share in the blame."

"All of us?"

"English soldiers do not carry plows to till the land, Miss Mallory, they carry guns and bayonets. English bullets, like English cannons, leave death and destruction in their wake. And the hapless peasants whose homes and countries are trapped between opposing forces have a difficult time remembering which side God is on."

She stared at him, her pretty forehead wrinkled with concern. "I . . . I had not thought of it in just that way."

"Of course you had not, and I am a beast to bring up such a weighty subject on such a sunny day."

"I pray you, sir, never apologize to me for speaking the truth. Nor for sharing your thoughts. You believe that all of life is precious, and those feelings do you justice. Even on a sunny day."

"Madam, you are very understanding. I had not meant to be such a sobersides. I suppose my past is not as far behind me as I had thought."

"Pasts never are," she said. "No matter how hard we may try to forget them, or how often we tell ourselves that they do not matter, the truth is that our pasts never leave us. They linger in our brains, spinning like miniature potter's wheels and constantly shaping our futures."

"That is it exactly! Which is why it is essential that we never forget those who fought and died—soldiers and civilian alike—for if we do, other Napoleons will come to power, and other generations will be sacrificed at the altar of their leaders' callousness. Politically ambitious men get us into wars because they take themselves too seriously, while not taking life seriously enough."

To his surprise, the lady reached over and placed her gloved hand atop his. She offered no platitudes, no glib hopes for the future, she merely let the pressure of her fingers speak for her.

David shifted the reins to his left hand, then he turned his right hand over, capturing her fingers in his larger grasp. After a moment, he lifted her hand to his lips and placed a kiss on her wrist, just above the hem of her glove. Her skin was firm, yet unbelievably smooth, and he let his lips linger there, enjoying the warmth of her, the clean, womanly fragrance of her, the vibrancy that sprang to life at his touch. "Olivia," he whispered.

"Yes?"

Her voice was not quite steady, and when David looked into her upturned face, he knew that she felt

what he felt, though the emotions were obviously new
to her, and perhaps a bit frightening.

"You are very beautiful."

"I am?"

"Oh, yes."

It was the truth, but it was not what he had meant
to say. Something told him that if he did and said all
he wanted to do and say, his gray-eyed country mouse
might well turn and flee in fear. Olivia might be five
and twenty by the calendar, but when it came to the
passions that drew a man to a woman, she was no
more worldly wise than that moonfaced miss riding in
Kitty Selby's landau. One might be forgiven for thinking that Olivia had spent her formative years in some
sort of emotional cocoon. "Did you?" he asked.

"Did I what?"

He had not realized he had spoken aloud, and he
snatched at the first subject that came to mind. "Your
nose," he said. "Did you know that it is just the slightest bit crooked?"

Her eyes widened in surprise. An instant later surprise turned to pique, and she pulled her hand free of
his. Not that he blamed her. "You think *my* nose is
crooked? Sir, do you not own a looking glass?"

At this, David threw back his head and laughed.
Heaven help him, but he loved it that she gave as good as
she got. "I do own a looking glass, madam. Fortunately, I
need look in it but once a day, and then for only those few
minutes required to keep my face clean-shaven."

He touched his forefinger to the tip of her nose,
and to his surprise, she did not pull away. "Surely,
Miss Mallory, you do not mean to equate this small,
slightly imperfect feature that is so charming in your
face with that battered one of mine?"

"It was you who introduced the subject."

"Only because I keep thinking how delightful it
would be to rain kisses across that small bridge."

"K-kisses?"

"Thousands of them. Until I was acquainted with every freckle."

"Freckles! Allow me to inform you, sir, that I do not have the first—"

"And once my lips had learned every detail of your nose," he said, interrupting her protestations, "I would set them to memorizing the feel of your eyelids . . . the soft, satiny curve of your cheek . . . the gentle bow of your upper lip."

His words were softly hypnotic, making Olivia feel deliciously light-headed. But more than that, she felt oddly satisfied, as if she had been waiting all her life to find the one man who wished to memorize her eyelids. "David," she said, her voice not quite steady, "I should like very much to have you rain k—"

"Crighton," Lord Selby called from the landau that was even then turning left into a pretty green area shaded by beech trees coppiced two centuries earlier. "We will stop here for a few minutes. There is a little brook just over that little hill, and Kitty is convinced Miss Mallory will like it prodigiously."

What Miss Mallory would like, Olivia thought, was to number among her friends those who did not bring her back down to earth at the very moment a marvelously handsome man was promising to take her to the stars. "How kind of Kitty," she called to the lady's husband.

"Yes, indeed," David said, the words spoken just above a whisper, "very kind. And should you wish to repay her, Miss Mallory, there is always your parasol. If you take careful aim, two or three good whacks should do the job."

True to his promise, Lord Selby insisted that the single ladies must not be monopolized. Captain Brougthern had declared himself happy to remain on his horse, but when the party began the final leg of their drive, Joel Windham had given over the reins of his cabriolet to Lieutenant Averill, who appeared inordinately pleased to have Esme beside him. Meanwhile, Olivia joined Kitty and Tristan in the landau, which left Miss Agnes Averill to ride with David in the curricle.

"Together by default," she said, half apologetically.

"True enough," David replied, holding his hand down to help her up, "but I hope you will not hold that against me."

She giggled. "Sir, you must know that I meant that *you* got *me* by default."

"Whatever the circumstance, Miss Averill, it need not follow that we cannot enjoy getting acquainted."

"Oh, no, my lord, for I should like to get to know you."

"Why, thank you, ma'am."

They rode for some minutes with the bulk of the conversation involving the beauty of the passing scenery. Since flirting with very young ladies was not in his style, David attempted to keep the topics innocuous; especially after he discovered that the likeable chit with the shy smile and the nice brown eyes was as guileless as a puppy. When he complimented her on the jasper green bonnet she wore, she informed him, quite artlessly, that it had been purchased only the previous morning. "And it was unbelievably dear. I spent my entire pin money."

"But such a pretty bonnet," he said, "is surely worth every last farthing."

When the young lady blushed, David changed the subject again, asking her how she was enjoying her stay in town.

"At first," she said, "all I wanted was to return to Cambridgeshire. My brother was very kind, taking me for drives in the park, and once to Astley's Amphitheater, but I missed my dog and my horse, and there was no one to talk to."

"But, as you say, that was at first. I collect the situation is no longer true."

"Not at all, my lord, for now I have met Esme, and I feel as though we have been friends forever. Though what I shall do when she goes home to St. Guilford, I do not know."

"When she goes home?" David tried to keep his voice noncommittal, but it was difficult when it hit him like a powerful fist to the solar plexus just how dull London would be without Olivia Mallory. "Have the ladies set a date for their return to Suffolk?"

"That I do not know. Originally they had planned to remain in town for only a fortnight, but something Esme said made me think their plans had changed. Something—or perhaps it is someone—has induced Miss Mallory to consider extending their stay."

Someone! David smiled, for surely that someone was him. Though not a conceited man, he knew that women found him every bit as attractive as he found them, and he knew as well that Olivia was too naive to dissemble. Furthermore, she was no tease, and she would not have touched his hand, then allowed him to kiss her wrist, if some other man was paying her court.

Not that David was paying her court exactly. True, she was beautiful, and he enjoyed being in her company—no, he more than enjoyed it, he looked forward to it—and he definitely wanted to press her delectable body against his and give her what he was certain would be her first kiss. At the moment, however, introducing the gray-eyed enchantress to a few of the pleasures of the flesh was as far as his thoughts had progressed.

"I believe Esme said her sister had met more than once with a gentleman on Holburn Street, but if she told me his name, I have forgotten it. Perhaps he is her reason for extending their stay."

Miss Agnes had continued to speak, but David, lost in his own thoughts, had not been attending. Now, he realized she had said something about a man. A man Olivia had met twice. Damn his eyes!

David knew a moment's desire to put his fist through the unknown man's face. It was a strange, new sensation, this wish to plant a facer on a person he had never met, and if he did not know it to be impossible, he might have thought he was jealous.

Now there was a preposterous notion!

David Crighton jealous? Never!

He had known many women, both as flirts and as mistresses, and any time a woman did not reciprocate his feelings, or if she tried to play him off against another man, David merely walked away. Life was too short, and there were too many beautiful women in the world to bother with game playing.

Damnation! Miss Averill was speaking again, and as before, he had missed everything she had said up until the moment she spoke Olivia's name. "Of course, it is possible that I misunderstood the entire thing. My brother says that I am sometimes a bit shatterbrained."

"The entire thing," David repeated, hoping to encourage her to explain her words. "And that would be?"

"About the book of poems."

David felt as confused as a man who comes upon a group of people speaking in a foreign language he cannot understand. "The book of poems?"

Miss Averill gave him a look that said quite clearly that she was surprised by his inability to follow a simple conversation. "The poems Miss Mallory wishes to have published. It was her reason for coming to town, after all, and Esme said that she—Miss Mallory, that is—was quite disappointed when the publisher wanted proof of something or other before he would agree to publish the book."

David stared at Agnes Averill, who prattled on about never having met a real poet before.

A poet? Olivia? Was Miss Averill crazy, or was he? "I think you must have misunderstood that part about the book," he said, "for Miss Mallory told me herself that she had no poetic ability whatsoever."

The girl turned red as a poppy, embarrassed to have something she had said questioned. "I . . . I do not *think* I am mistaken, my lord. In fact, I am persuaded that I am not, for Esme said Miss Mallory's penmanship is so bad that she—Esme—had been obliged to copy the poems so the publisher could read them."

The Selbys' coachman had turned the landau onto a narrow lane, and David followed suit, his smooth handling of his horses not giving the least indication of the turmoil inside his brain. Olivia had told him she was no poet. In fact, she had laughed at the suggestion that she was in the least creative. "I am of the 'roses are red, violets are blue' variety," she had said. "And even then I have difficulty rhyming the third line."

David had laughed when she said it, amused by her self-deprecating remarks. It would appear, however, that the lady had lied to him. Though why she should deem it necessary to concoct such a Banbury tale, he could not even guess. Was the charming little ruse meant merely to keep him from asking further questions? And if so, why?

He was being foolish, he told himself. Becoming suspicious without cause. Obviously he had spent too many years gathering information for the Office of Foreign Affairs, for it had made him distrustful. Or perhaps it was this business of the dead cat sent to his uncle that had David seeing duplicity where it could not possibly exist.

And yet, Olivia had asked about those poetry societies. And she was acquainted with Sir Arthur Hix, a man David had every reason to distrust. A man his uncle had every reason to view with abhorrence.

Could Olivia Mallory be playing some sort of devious game? She and Sir Arthur Hix? In view of his uncle's current problems, it was imperative that David find out. And he *would* find out. Of that there could be no doubt, for he was very good at ferreting out information others wished to keep hidden.

In light of the fact that for the past few years he had loosened the tongues of some of Napoleon's most devious agents—men whose very lives depended upon their ability to keep a secret—discovering what Olivia Mallory was hiding should be a simple matter. As easy as taking sweets from a baby.

Richmond village was only slightly larger than its neighbor, the village of Wimbledon, but it was not that particular distinction that made it a favorite with Londoners seeking a bit of fresh air. Nor was it the magnificence of Richmond Palace, which had figured as a royal seat as far back as the twelfth century. What Londoners came by the thousands to see was the beautiful park, with its majestic oak trees, its wide expanses of rolling greenswards, and its fields of colorful wildflowers.

The land, which ran along the Thames from Kew to Richmond, then rose up to the park, had been a royal chase for centuries, and roaming free in the more than two thousand acres of sumptuous landscape were all manner of fauna. Birds flew in and out among the trees, while on the ground badgers and hedgehogs scurried about, giving brief glimpses of their usually secretive lives. Principal among the wildlife, though, were the herds of red and fallow deer—herds that had grown so thick they could be seen around almost every turn, grazing without fear of the visitors.

While the Selbys' capable servants put the final touches to the alfresco tables, arranging the fine linens, silver, china, and crystal with a formality they knew their master and mistress would expect, Kitty and her guests paused at a little hillock known as

"King Henry's Mount." The site commanded an impressive stretch of the Thames Valley, and on a clear day the view was said to be nearly panoramic, extending from Windsor Castle to the dome of St. Paul's Cathedral.

"Legend has it," their hostess informed them, "that Henry VIII stood at this very spot, watching for a rocket to rise from Tower Hill, signaling the beheading of his second wife, Anne Boleyn."

"Was it a success?" Agnes Averill asked.

When everyone stared at her, open-mouthed, she flushed scarlet, then hurried to explain that she meant the firing of the rocket, not the beheading.

Everyone laughed, and Lieutenant Averill breathed an audible sigh. "For a minute there," he said, "I feared I would be obliged to say something intelligent, just to uphold the family honor."

"Now there was a narrow escape," offered his friend, Captain Brougthern, "for I have known you at least three years, and I have never heard you say anything even remotely intelligent."

After that, the teasing began in earnest. While the military gentlemen vied to see who could be the most insulting, Kitty put her arm through Augusta Crighton's, then invited the rest of the ladies to follow her to the site of the alfresco breakfast.

"Oh, my!" Esme said upon first seeing the "rustic" table settings, complete with place cards arranged in little silver filigree holders. "I had no idea it would be so elegant."

"Nor I," Agnes echoed. "To own the truth, I still suspect my eyes are playing tricks on me."

Three tables—one with chairs stationed around it, one to hold the more than two dozen covered dishes, and one for the cellarets containing the dozen bottles of champagne—were situated on a lovely stretch of lawn within sight of the famous Stone Lodge. The lodge, a Palladian-style house with a graceful staircase and stately pillars, was built of Portland stone, which made it almost blindingly white in the sun. Still, it could not rival the crisp, white gloves of the twelve servants who stood at attention, ready to wait upon the nine guests.

Of the nine, Olivia's dining partners were Mr. Denholm Crighton, who sat to her right, and Captain Brougthern, who sat to her left. David Crighton was directly across from her, but thanks to a large silver vase that had been filled with tall shoots of yellow-budded forsythia and fragrant lilacs then placed in the center of the table, she would have needed to be a contortionist to see him, never mind engage him in conversation.

Good manners decreed that she divide her time between conversing with the partner on her right and the partner on her left. Unfortunately, Mr. Denholm Crighton did not hold up his end of the conversation. He spoke only when spoken to, and then in monosyllables; and yet, Olivia had the wholly unsubstantiated belief that it was sadness, not rudeness, that kept him silent. His thoughts seemed many miles away, as though happiness for him lay in the past.

Augusta Crighton sat on the other side of the captain, which made it impossible for Olivia to take any part in the quiet conversation the lady held with Lord Selby, who was on her left. It occurred to Olivia that Mrs. Crighton was not a happy woman, but there was a difference between her unhappiness and her husband's sadness. What the difference might be, Olivia could not say.

They were an enigma, the Crightons. Though what possible business that was of hers, she dare not ask herself. If she did, she might have to admit that she was half in love with their nephew.

The thought had come unbidden, and it caused Olivia to choke on a sip of champagne. With shaking hands, she returned the crystal to the table, afraid she might break it, or do something equally foolish. Clearly she was not to be trusted with fine crystal or strong spirits, for her mind was obviously deranged. Why else would she fancy herself in love with David Crighton?

Why, she knew nothing of the man except that he made her heart race and her breathing labored, and that every minute spent in his company was more exciting than the last. But were her affections engaged? Were his?

Surely it was too soon for either of them to have formed an attachment. And yet, something had happened between them that very first moment, when their gazes had met across the lobby of Grillon's. Something magical.

But was it magic? Or was it merely an illusion? Was it . . . could it be love?

That last question seemed oddly familiar, and with a start, Olivia realized that Cousin Jane had used almost the same words when writing in her diary about her friend, the mysterious poet, "D."

Thankfully, Olivia's attention was claimed by Captain Brougthern, allowing her to push from her mind this very startling coincidence of phrase. The captain, whose plate had been piled high with sliced ham, asparagus in an aspic, and broiled perch in a wine sauce, asked her how she liked the fish. "First rate, don't you think?"

She had eaten very little other than an asparagus spear and a few bites of green beans, but just to be polite she cut off a small bite of the fish and raised her fork to her mouth. After swallowing the spicy concoction, she smiled at the captain. "Very nice, indeed, sir."

The military gentleman's champagne glass had been refilled a number of times, and when he spoke to Olivia again, his voice was slightly slurred. "Do you not think, ma'am, that someone should make a toast to our host and hostess?"

"But not you," Joel Windham said from across the table, "for you will prose on forever."

"Then who?" the captain asked. "It cannot come from you, Windham, for the lady is your sister."

"What we need," Lieutenant Averill said, "is a poet. Someone with a gift for words."

"What about Miss Mallory?" the gentleman's sister asked.

All eyes turned from Agnes Averill to Olivia, and as everyone waited expectantly for Olivia's response, she began to sympathize with a bug trapped between two pieces of glass so it could be examined under a microscope. "There has been some sort of mistake," she said, "for I assure you, I possess no talent with words."

"Come now," David Crighton said, his voice all but disembodied behind the tall flowers in the silver vase, "you are among friends here, Miss Mallory. Let us have no displays of maidenly modesty."

Maidenly modesty! Olivia tried not to take offense at the words, but there was something in his tone—some undeniable edginess—that made her wonder if he was angry with her.

"Were the number of my friends legion, Lord Crighton, I would still be obliged to refuse. And the refusal is based not on modesty, but on reality. Now, sir, I pray you let the matter rest."

An awkward silence followed, causing Olivia to wish she could slip to the ground and hide beneath the flowing linen of the tablecloth. That possibility denied her, she stared straight ahead, seeing nothing but her own reflection in the silver vase.

Kitty, ever the good hostess, stepped into the breech. "If our praises must be sung, which I am persuaded is not at all necessary, let the words come from a true poet. There is one among us who possesses an unquestioned gift, for he—"

"By Jove!" Joel Windham said, "you are right, Kitty. Don't know how I came to forget." Smiling, he turned to David. "What say you, Crighton? Surely you can give us a good toast. After all, if what my brother-in-law says of you is true, you were once known as 'The Bard of Eton.'"

Chapter Nine

*T*he Bard of Eton.

Olivia heard no more. It was as if a witch from one of the fairy tales had dropped some sort of invisible dome over her, enclosing her in a shield of impenetrable glass. She could neither hear nor see, and for a time her senses were in such a state of shock that she could not even feel.

He was a poet. David.

No! She refused to give the least credence to the thoughts that were invading her brain like vandals bent on destroying her sanity. It was all just a coincidence. After all, millions of people wrote poetry. Just as millions of people had names that began with the letter "D."

And yet . . .

As if to give her mind something else to think about, her stomach began to roil. Wondering if she were about to make a spectacle of herself, she swallowed, then swallowed again, willing herself not to be sick. Her temples began to pound; then, as if from some distant place, she watched as David Crighton stood and began to speak. She heard nothing of his toast, but when he lifted his glass and everyone else lifted theirs, she followed suit, though she could not bring herself to take even one sip of the sparkling liquid.

The Bard of Eton. With such an epithet, it stood to
reason the man would possess a degree of talent. Kitty
had said his was an "unquestioned gift." Was it? Was
it enough to make a lonely spinster fancy herself in
love with him?

Olivia certainly had. Not twenty minutes ago she
had admitted to being half in love with David
Crighton . . . admitted it in words that were almost
identical to those she had read in her cousin's diary.
Secret words written in Jane's own hand.

Poor Jane. She had fallen in love through letters
and poems, without having the least idea how handsome her poet was. How charming he could be. How
those dark blue eyes could look so deep into a woman's eyes that she felt as if he were seeing all the way
to her soul.

Hurt, anger, and a feeling of betrayal warred inside
Olivia, making her long to stand and knock aside the
blasted vase of flowers—knock it aside and demand
that David deny knowing Jane Frant. Demand that he
deny making Jane fall in love with him. Oh, how she
needed to hear him say it was not true! She wanted
him to look into her eyes and tell her that he was not
the man who had written those poems and letters to
her cousin.

She wanted him to tell her that he was no poet. If
he could look at her and say it, then she might be
able to put aside all her doubts. True, he had offered
to assist Olivia to find the poetry societies, and he had
become rather cool when she mentioned meeting Sir
Arthur Hix. Of course, anyone might know about the
societies, but would anyone other than another poet
recognize Sir Arthur's name?

No, no, no! It could not be true. David Crighton
was not some base character, some philanderer. He
could not be.

She recalled that spark that had ignited between her
and David at their first meeting. Surely such an instant

and indisputable attraction meant that something special radiated from his soul to hers. Surely it indicated that *she* was as special to him as he was to her.

"I love the ladies too much." Those were David's own words. He had said them not more than two hours ago, and Olivia had laughed. She was not laughing now.

"Miss Mallory," Captain Brougthern said, "are you feeling quite the thing?"

Mortified to think she might be laying her emotions out for everyone to see, Olivia said, "I . . . I do not know what you mean, sir."

"I vow, ma'am, I am beginning to wish I had not eaten that broiled perch."

His voice seemed to come from a long way off, and a moment later, when Olivia tried to reply, her words came out a thready whisper.

"Brougthern," Joel said from across the table, "is something amiss? You look in rather queer stirrups, old fellow."

"I say, Miss Esme," Lieutenant Averill said, "your sister does not appear at all well either. In fact, she's looking decidedly down-pin."

Olivia tried to tell the gentleman that she was just fine. Unfortunately, while she struggled to form the words, spots began to dance before her eyes, and before she quite knew what was happening, she slipped slowly to the ground.

"Fainted!" Olivia attempted to push aside the wet linen napkin her sister held to her forehead. "Do not be absurd, Esme. I have never fainted in my life."

"Be that as it may, Livvy, unless you have some other name for it, you fainted."

"But—"

To put an end to the discussion, Esme opened up the napkin and placed it over Olivia's entire face. "Have it your way, Livvy, for I am much too fond of you to argue with you when you are at a disadvantage. However, if you did not faint, I wish you will explain to me why you were lying about on the lawn."

Olivia groaned. "Am I still on the ground?"

"No, you are not. While the others saw to poor Captain Brougthern, who was casting up his accounts in a most distressing manner, Joel carried you to Lady Selby's landau. That is where we are now. And as soon as you feel strong enough, his lordship has said we may return to town."

"His lordship?" Olivia did not want to ride with David in his curricle, nor did she have the strength to explain to Esme that she needed time before she faced him again. "Not David," she said. "Please."

"No, no," Esme replied, "I should have said Lord Selby. As it happens, Lord Crighton has offered to take Captain Brougthern back to the barracks, with Lieutenant Averill riding along the curricle on the chance that assistance is needed."

"And Miss Averill?"

"She will ride with Joel. No one else became unwell, praise heaven, for only you and the captain ate the fish. We were all very worried, and as you can imagine, Lady Selby is beside herself with embarrassment."

Hoping to relieve Kitty's mind, Olivia removed the obscuring damp napkin and sat up, though her reward for such foolish bravado was blurred vision and a head that threatened to spin right off her shoulders. It required great fortitude to remain upright, but after several minutes she began to feel more the thing.

When her vision cleared, she looked around for Kitty—at least, she told herself she searched for Kitty. Actually, the first person she spied was David Crighton, who stood beside his curricle, presumably waiting for Captain Brougthern to say he was ready to travel. His uncle, Mr. Denholm Crighton, stood beside him, and though they were much too far away for Olivia to hear what they said, the two men appeared deep in conversation.

"I am quite certain," Denholm Crighton said, giving his nephew a questioning look, "that I have never met Miss Mallory before today. Nor have I ever heard her name mentioned. Why do you ask, dear boy?"

"Just an idle thought, Uncle. Nothing more."

"Are you certain? Somehow, I got the impression the young lady might be of special importance to you. Was I correct? Is she special, or are you merely experiencing pangs of remorse for having called attention to her when she was feeling ill?"

If his uncle only knew!

Remorse did not begin to describe David's feelings, for he could not believe the rude manner in which he had spoken to Olivia. Not only was it ungentlemanly to accuse a lady of exhibiting false modesty, it was unforgivable to confront her while seated at a dinner party—unforgivable and completely unprofessional. He had behaved like a rank amateur, for a good operative did not gather information by attacking the person in possession of all the answers. The adage was still true about catching more flies with honey than with vinegar.

Another old adage was equally true, the one about pride going before a fall. Earlier, David had been positive that discovering what Olivia was hiding would be as easy as taking sweets from a baby. More fool he, for the "baby" did not relinquish her secrets as easily as he had hoped.

Whatever she was, Olivia Mallory was no fool, and David had overplayed his hand by trying to make her confess to something she meant to keep hidden. All he had succeeded in doing was forfeiting the element of surprise. Furthermore, even if she had given the toast to their host and hostess, spouting sonnet after sonnet, the demonstration would have proven only one thing, that she was a poet. It would not have explained her reasons for lying about the matter. Nor would it have confirmed or denied her possible connection with the letters and the gruesome "gifts" being sent to his uncle.

As for the helpless feeling that had gripped David's insides when he had first noticed Olivia's ashen face, then watched her slowly fall to the ground, he did not even want to think about that. He felt sympathy for the captain, of course, for he was clearly the sicker of the two. Still, it was not the same as seeing a lady become ill in public. David could just imagine how embarrassed she must be.

"No," he replied at last, when he realized his uncle was still waiting for an answer to his question, "the young lady is of no special importance to me."

"Well, then," Denholm Crighton said, "I shall say no more on the subject. Instead, I believe I will find your aunt, so we may return to town. I did not wish to come today, and the only reason I agreed was because you insisted. As it is, if there is anything good to be said for this entire outing, it is that only two of the guests chose the fish. And, of course, we are most fortunate that the servants would not have eaten until later. They, at least, were spared the captain's fate."

"No matter the outcome of the day, Uncle, I am glad you came. You should get out more."

The suggestion seemed to annoy his usually mild-mannered relative, for he turned quickly, all affability gone from his face. "And perhaps, Nephew, you and everyone else should mind your own damn business and leave me to mind mine."

David could not have been more surprised if a floppy-eared hare had suddenly stood on his hind legs and growled like a bear. "Your pardon, Uncle. I assure you I never meant to intrude. I am merely concerned for your welfare, and—"

"Keep your concern. I neither need nor want it. All I want is to be left alone!"

David watched in stunned silence as his uncle turned and walked away, the quiet gentleman angrier than he had ever seen him.

"Damnation!" Tristan Selby said, coming up just as Denholm Crighton all but shouted his desire to be left alone. "Whatever you said to make your uncle so livid, old fellow, I wish you had saved it for another time. Poor Kitty is as close to tears as I have ever seen her, what with the fish having gone off, and two guests having become ill. And though I cannot expect a bachelor to appreciate the strain such a day imposes on a woman in Kitty's condition, I can assure you that she does not need to have this fiasco crowned with a family squabble."

It was obviously David's day to have mild-mannered men turn on him, for Tristan was not finished. "Can't figure what has gotten into you today, Crighton. For a man with your reputation for subtlety and tact, you have been unconscionably churlish. Not to put too fine a point on it, my friend, you have made a complete ass of yourself."

"At least you still call me friend."

Lord Selby put up his fists in mock threat, as if he might draw his friend's cork. "For now," he said. "But what I still cannot understand is why you embarrassed Miss Mallory in that boorish manner, all but demanding that she make a toast. Why, if anyone had asked me earlier, I would have said you were interested in her. Especially after putting Kitty to all that trouble just so you could meet the lady."

"Believe me, Tristan, I have no excuse for my actions, and I beg you will make my apologies to Kitty."

"What of your apologies to Miss Mallory? Why, if you were ten years younger, old boy, I would suspect you had thought the lady was perfect, and that she had seriously disappointed you by being human."

*   *   *

"What a disappointment," Esme said when she
came from Olivia's bedchamber with the little tray still
bearing the pot of tea and the plate of toasted bread.
"She has rejected every offer of food. I had hoped
that after her nap she would be hungry, but she says
the very thought of food, no matter how bland, makes
her ill."

Hepzebah took the tray and set it on the console
table beside the suite door. "I'll not take it down just
yet. Miss Livvy may wake later and want a bite of
something."

"I hope she sleeps through the night," replied her
sister, "for I am exhausted, and in exactly two minutes
I mean to be in my own bed, fast asleep." After em-
phasizing her words with a wide yawn, Esme bid the
maid a good night, then followed through with her
vow to go directly to bed.

The hour having just gone nine, Hepzebah was not
yet ready to retire. She planned to sit beside the fire
a bit longer, for one of her best stockings had a hole
in the toe and needed to be darned, and the lace on
one of Esme's petticoats needed mending. At some
point, the quietness of the room and the warmth of
the fire must have had their way with the maid, for
she dozed off, only to be awakened with a start when
she thought she heard someone open the suite door,
then close it again immediately, being careful to make
as little noise as possible.

"What . . . who?" Because the small ormolu clock
on the mantel had begun to chime eleven, she told
herself it was the chimes that had awakened her.
"Reckon I imagined that about the door being
opened."

Though she was convinced she had dreamed the
stealthy noise, before she banked the fire and blew
out the work candles, Hepzebah turned the large brass
key in the lock, securing the suite against intruders,

real or imagined. "Lunnon's a wicked city," she said, "happen I should start locking the door of an evening."

From her bedchamber, Olivia heard the mantel clock in the sitting room chime eleven, then there was the unmistakable sound of Hepzebah talking to herself, a thing the servant had taken to doing more often since they arrived in town. Poor Hepzebah. She was a country woman to her very soul, and except for the footman who had invited her to Green Park on Sunday, she had found little to admire in London.

Considering her own miserable experiences that day, Olivia wondered if she would ever like the place again. She groaned, an understandable reaction when she recalled the events of the afternoon. Had there ever been such an alfresco breakfast? She hoped not.

She might have withstood the food poisoning well enough had she not already been suffering from the shock of discovering that David Crighton was a poet. "The Bard of Eton," Joel Windham had called him.

Olivia shut her eyes, but after having been abed for seven hours, she felt certain she would not soon go back to sleep; especially not with the questions about David going around and around in her head. Since there was one obvious place where she might find answers, she decided that now would be a good time to return to Cousin Jane's diary. If she were lucky, Jane might have called her poet-friend by his full name in the later pages.

If she were luckier still, the name would not be David.

After lighting her bedside candle, Olivia went to the little cherry Davenport desk and slid back the green leather-covered top. The Morocco diary lay just as she had left it, along with the small key Jane had worn on a gold chain around her neck. After unlocking the clasp, Olivia found the place where she had stopped reading two days ago and started anew.

As before, she felt a trespasser, or worse, reading words never meant to be seen by anyone but the author. And yet, if she wanted to know the name of the poet—and she wanted to know it now more than ever—there was no other way. The information in the diary held the only possible clues.

On almost every page, Cousin Jane rhapsodized about the beauty of the words written by her friend. According to Jane, he was the most gifted poet of the age, just as he was the kindest, the most sensitive, the most worthy of admiration and love.

> *My friend tells me that it is my friendship alone that sustains him, for none but another poet can understand a poet's dreams. A poet's hopes. A poet's disappointments.*
>
> *He tells me that life would lose its flavor if I should cease to be his friend and muse. This I readily understand, for I feel exactly the same. Knowing he is in this world is sufficient to inspire my own poems. I do not think I have ever been as productive, as creative, as I have been since he came into my life.*

The next few pages of the diary were filled with the day-to-day running of Frant House, with only one slightly interesting notation.

> *I asked my father if I might take my cousins to town for a bit of a holiday. Poor Livvy's one season in town was cut short by the deaths of my aunt and uncle, and though she has never complained—she is such a dear, sweet girl—I know she must still feel the disappointment. As for darling little Esme, my friend says the little girl would love the wax museum and the shows at Astley's Amphitheater.*

Naturally, I want so badly to finally meet my friend, and he wishes to meet me face-to-face.

The entry for the following day was short and terse.

Father said he would give prayerful consideration to the matter of my taking the girls to London for a holiday, but when I awoke this morning, he had slipped a note beneath my bedchamber door saying he—not God, but he—did not think it a good idea.

I have never been so miserable in my life. Or so angry. I realize it is my duty to be obedient, but what harm could there be in a spinster no longer youthful taking two young girls on holiday?

Olivia shut the diary with an angry snap. That arrogant, self-absorbed martinet! How dare he deny his daughter's one request. Obedient! Nuns in a cloistered convent were allowed more latitude.

Olivia grew even more upset as she was besieged by memories of incidents she had overlooked as a girl. There was the time after Sunday services when Jane had lingered more than a few moments exchanging greetings with the rector and his wife. Uncle Raeford had stood near the gate to the churchyard, quietly staring at his daughter. He had not uttered a word, but that quiet stare told Jane more profoundly than an entire barrage of words ever could that her father did not approve of such "trivial" socializing.

Not that he ever argued, or raised his voice, that was not Raeford Frant's way. He simply refused to acknowledge any opinion other than his own or that of the Heavenly Father. And when it came to God's wishes, it was understood that only Uncle Raeford possessed sufficient understanding to interpret those.

With memories flooding back to her, Olivia was appalled at how confined and narrow poor Jane's life had been. Not only had Raeford Frant's notions of propriety prohibited his daughter from having innocent friendships in the village, his conviction that he knew best positively robbed her of her right to an opinion or a thought of her own.

No wonder Jane fell in love with a man who existed only in the lines of his letters and his poetry. As long as her correspondence remained a secret, her father could not force her to end it—for her own good, of course. As long as Raeford Frant did not know about "D," he could not demand that his daughter give up the one thing in her life that had brought her happiness.

Olivia was not certain she believed in the actual existence of a fiery, sulphurous afterlife, but if there was a hell, she hoped it contained an especially hot corner reserved for domestic despots.

She opened the diary once again. Even though she had been reading for at least an hour by a single candle, and her eyes felt dry and taxed with the strain to see, Olivia could not stop now, not with such anger in her heart. She must know how her cousin, a sensible, responsible woman of thirty-seven, dealt with her disappointment at not being allowed to go to London.

When she turned to the next day's entry, a single sheet of paper, obviously folded and refolded hundreds of times, fell to the floor. Curious, Olivia retrieved the sheet, then unfolded it carefully, lest the fragile pieces break apart in her hands. It was a letter to her cousin.

My dear, dear friend,

I share your disappointment, for I had so wanted to see you—to sit with you over a cozy tea, as friends do.

How I longed to look into your eyes, eyes you

*call "indifferent" blue, while I choose to think of
them as resembling the clear, delicate blue of the
unpretentious campion that grows near my home
in the north.*

*It is my favorite flower, and thoughts of it feed
my soul. Just as thoughts of you feed my heart.*

*It is a myth that in his three-score years and
ten, a man can love but one woman. One might
as well say that a flower once planted in one garden can never bloom again in some other.*

*My dear friend, my cherished "campion," you
have made my spirit bloom again.*

*Your devoted,
"D"*

On the reverse of the letter was a poem, dedicated
to "That campion who is my muse."

*Blue campions grew amid the gray stone wall,
But I had no time for such and passed them by.
I sped to answer fame and fortune's call,
And now there are no campions, and I cry.*

Olivia refolded the letter and returned it to the
diary, and this time when she closed the Morocco-
bound book that revealed the very heart and soul of
a dear cousin, she closed it with reverence. This book
and the poems were all that remained of a woman
who once loved and was loved in return, and no one—
especially not the interloper into whose care the book
had come—had the right to sit in judgment of Jane
Frant or of the man she loved.

"But please," she begged of heaven, "do not let
that man be David Crighton. I do not think I could
endure it if David turned out to be Jane's beloved
'D.'"

Chapter Ten

"*O*h, Miss Mallory," Mr. George Vickers called to Olivia as she crossed Grillon's lobby, "a moment if you please."

Olivia paused, she could hardly do otherwise, and waited until the reed-thin concierge reached her. She hoped he would not detain her for long, for Esme had taken forever to choose a dress and bonnet she felt appropriate to wear to a poetry reading, and if they did not get a hackney right away, they would be late. Since Thursday afternoons were the only time ladies were invited to the readings, Olivia did not wish to call attention to herself by being the last to arrive.

"Yes, Mr. Vickers?"

The concierge bid her a good afternoon. "I did not see you yesterday, Miss Mallory, or I would have spoken to you then."

"Yes, Mr. Vickers?"

"I thought you might wish to know that a gentleman stopped by on Tuesday, asking if I would send his card up to your suite. Naturally, I did not make him privy to the information that you and Miss Esme were guests of Lord and Lady Selby. I merely informed him that you were absent from the hotel for the day."

Thinking the man who called might be Mr. Quartermaine, the publisher, Olivia asked if there was a message.

The concierge shook his head ever so carefully, so as not to disarrange the meticulously combed hair that did not quite conceal his receding hairline. Satisfied that he was still presentable, he reached inside his coat and removed a calling card from the small pocket of his waistcoat. "The gentleman left only this."

A glance at the white pasteboard revealed an engraved name embellished with curlicues. The name was Arthur Hix, Bart., and as quickly as Olivia read it, she returned the card to Mr. Vickers. "I have no wish to receive this gentleman, so if he should call again, I depend upon you, sir, to inform him that I am not at home to visitors."

The concierge turned several shades of red, and though he might have been embarrassed at the thought of turning away a baronet, he knew his duty to the ladies and gentlemen who were guests of the hotel. "It shall be as you wish, Miss Mallory."

Olivia gave him what she hoped was a reassuring smile. "Thank you, Mr. Vickers. I knew I could depend upon you."

Remembering the offensive little man at the poetry society on Carnaby Street, Olivia entered the Lexington Street society with no great expectations of a chivalrous welcome from its members. As it turned out, she could not have been more wrong, for of the twenty or so gentlemen seated at the refectory tables crowded into the ground-floor meeting room, not one of them appeared to object to having two ladies join them. In fact, when she and Esme first entered the meeting room, a middle-aged gentleman stood and escorted them to an empty table near the front. He even went so far as to bow to them politely and bid them welcome.

The sisters had only just gotten settled when Sir Arthur Hix entered from a side room. Exhibiting more formality than seemed necessary for so informal a group, the baronet took his place behind the polished mahogany lectern. Then, more like an actor on the stage than the president of a poetry society, he rapped twice with his gavel and called the meeting to order. He had dressed for the occasion in formal afternoon wear of gray breeches and blue coat, and a blue silk cravat had replaced the spotted Belcher handkerchief he had worn before. Even his rather longish Brutus hairstyle appeared to have benefited from the ministrations of a barber. All things considered, he looked quite distinguished, though when he spied Olivia and smiled, she experienced that same creepy sensation she had felt before.

"Is that him?" Esme whispered.

At Olivia's nod, the irrepressible chit grimaced. "No wonder you did not wish him to call upon you. What a man milliner."

"Shh," Olivia said, giving her sister a warning look that left no room for misinterpretation.

If anyone heard Esme, they were polite enough to pretend otherwise. After all, Sir Arthur was the president of the society.

In about ten minutes, when the announcements were at an end, the floor was opened to anyone who wished to come forward and read from their own or anyone else's work, being careful, of course, to give the author's name where appropriate. Olivia had not known what to expect in the way of participation, but before the meeting was over, at least half the gentlemen in attendance had taken advantage of the invitation, some reading with confidence while others stuttered and stammered, often getting off to false starts.

Thankfully, each speaker was limited to fifteen minutes at the lectern, for most of the original poetry was excruciatingly bad. So bad, in fact, that it was not long before Olivia understood why Mr. Quartermaine had seen promise in Jane Frant's poems. As for the creations of the unknown "D," not one of the published poems read that day was superior to his. Nor did any of the authors represented have names beginning with that initial.

The poetry readings lasted for three hours, a fact Olivia had not suspected earlier, or she might have thought better of attending, and by the time Sir Arthur returned to the lectern to say that time was up, Olivia felt as if her derriere had turned to a block of wood. After joining in the smattering of applause, she stood, caught Esme's arm, then turned to make her way toward the door. Unfortunately, Sir Arthur called to her, and she was obliged to stop and allow him to join her.

"Well," he said, after bowing to Olivia and acknowledging the introduction to Esme—an introduction Olivia could not avoid, "what did you think of our little group of artists, Miss Mallory? Was the poetry not exceptional?"

She might not like the baronet, but good manners dictated that she not voice her true opinion of the afternoon's reading. "Quite honestly, Sir Arthur, I have never been privy to so much poetry in one sitting, and I find my senses positively overwhelmed. I am persuaded I shall require a number of hours of solitude to allow the experience to permeate my consciousness."

"Me too," Esme added rather quickly. "A *number* of hours."

"Right you are, young lady," said an elderly gentleman who appeared to have been waiting for the moment when he might enter the conversation without appearing to interrupt. "Poetry is like fine wine. It is to be sipped, not gulped."

Considering the man's age, and the fact that Sir Arthur had bowed low to the white-haired gentleman, then stepped aside, Olivia smiled, acknowledging her willingness to be introduced. Truth to tell, she was eager to speak to anyone who succeeded in relieving her of the baronet's presence.

"Forgive an old man for being forward," he said, bowing to Olivia, "but I believe I saw you in the park the other day, conversing with my old friend, Mr. George Rice."

"The gentleman on the beautiful horse? Of course, sir."

"George told me," he continued, "that you are the granddaughter of General Sir Inago Mallory."

"I—that is *my sister* and I are, sir. Did you know our grandfather?"

"Inago and I were at school together, at least a thousand years ago. In fact, I knew your father and mother as well. Bad luck their meeting with such an untimely end."

Olivia thanked him for his belated condolences, then turned the subject back to General Mallory, asking the elderly gentleman to tell them a little of the grandfather they never knew.

The old gentleman related one or two schoolboy stories, apparently enjoying the reminiscences as much as the sisters enjoyed hearing of their grandfather. His speech was a bit blunt, but he kept the line and was vastly entertaining, and within a matter of minutes Esme was flirting outrageously with him. "You know who we are," she said, "but so far you have managed to keep your own identity a secret. That makes me wonder, sir, if you are someone whose acquaintance we should eschew. It would not surprise me in the least to discover that you are a notorious highwayman poet—a dastardly fellow whose very presence at this gathering puts him in danger of imminent arrest."

Sir Arthur, who had remained in the background, listening to their conversation, gasped. The white-haired gentleman merely laughed, however, then reached out and pinched Esme's cheek. "You are a saucy minx, young lady, and I will wager you have half the bucks in town beating a path to your door."

"La, sir," she replied, batting her eyelashes like the veriest ninnyhammer, "how could that be, when I have not *met* half the—"

"Not 'sir,'" the baronet said, the word hissed very close to Esme's ear.

"What?" Esme asked.

His face red with embarrassment, Sir Arthur Hix bowed once again to the older gentleman. "I beg your grace's pardon. Pray allow me to introduce Miss Mallory and Miss Esme Mallory. Young ladies, this is His Grace, the Duke of Thornborough."

After a moment of stunned silence, the sisters made deep curtsies. "Your grace," Olivia said.

Following that bit of brilliant repartee, she seemed to lose all ability to speak. As for Esme, the cat had apparently gotten her once-flirtatious tongue, for she merely stared, her eyes wide with astonishment. Thankfully, another gentleman claimed the duke's attention before either of the Mallorys embarrassed themselves beyond redemption, and they were required to do no more than bow when his grace bid them a good afternoon.

For the next few minutes, Olivia stood as if turned to stone, and only gradually did she become aware of a conversation taking place just behind her. "I had wanted to read it before the society," a very young man said, "but when I would have raised my hand to request time at the lectern, I felt my knees begin to knock against each other."

"Nerves," his slightly older companion said. "They can happen to anyone. First time I read before the society, my hands shook so badly the rattling of the paper positively drowned out my words." After a good laugh at his own expense, he said, "Here, let me have a look at what you brought."

"You do not mind?"

"Of course not. Always happy to hear a good poem." The man fell silent, obviously reading to himself, then a moment later, he said, "Ah, yes, I know this one well. Short but meaningful, 'The Blue Campion.' "

Olivia supposed it was the shock of having met the Duke of Thornborough that made her react so boldly, but she turned to the two young gentleman. "Did you say 'The Blue Campion'?"

"Yes, ma'am," the second man replied politely. "Are you familiar with the poem?"

"Perhaps. I am not certain. There might be two by that name."

To her surprise, the man began to read aloud. " 'Blue campions grew amid the gray stone wall,' " he said, " 'But I had no time for such and passed them by.' "

Olivia did not need to hear the final two lines, for she already knew them. She had read them for the first time two nights ago, when the folded paper fell out of Cousin Jane's diary.

When the young man was finished reading, he looked at Olivia. "Is it the poem you know, ma'am?"

She nodded, for she had been rendered nearly speechless by the unexpectedness of hearing "D's" words spoken, and she found her own words all but sticking in her throat. "I wonder, sir, could you . . . would you be so good as to tell me the name of the poet who penned those lines?"

"*I* can tell you that," Sir Arthur said.

When Olivia turned to look at the prissy little baronet, his mouth was set in a hard line, and his washed-out blue eyes were filled with an anger so intense, so hot she felt it physically, like a blast from a baker's oven. "The poem is mine," he said. "I wrote it."

Chapter Eleven

*I*f Olivia lived to be an old crone of a hundred, she would never forget the shock of hearing Sir Arthur Hix claim to be the writer of that poem. Immediately she was torn by dichotomous feelings. On the one hand, she was relieved to know that David Crighton was not "D," the man Jane Frant had loved. Yet on the other hand, she could not bear the thought of her dear cousin having fallen in love with a man as repugnant as Sir Arthur Hix.

Was "D" the initial of one of his other given names? And why, at their first meeting, when she allowed him to read one of the poems sent to Jane, had he told her that he had no idea who had written it?

No! she told herself, she did not even want to know the answers, and without another word to anyone, she took her sister's arm and all but pulled the chit from the room.

"Livvy!" Esme said, once they were outside, where no one could overhear them. "For the love of heaven, what has gotten into you? You did not even allow me time to bow to his grace, who must think us totally lacking in manners."

Unable to tell her sister the true reason for her peculiar behavior, she said, "It is of no consequence, for I doubt we shall ever see the duke again."

In this assumption she was totally mistaken, for

early the next morning a card of invitation was deliv-
ered to the suite by a liveried footman, a card from
Lady White, the daughter-in-law of the Duke of
Thornborough. In beautifully scripted copperplate, the
marchioness requested the presence of the Misses
Mallory at tea that afternoon.

"Oh, Livvy! How marvelous. Tea with a real marchioness. I cannot believe our good fortune. But what
shall we wear? Have we anything suitable? Oh, I know
I shall die of excitement!"

Naturally, there was no question of their refusing
so flattering an invitation, though Olivia was certain
that no matter what she wore, she would look an absolute hag. Considering the fact that she had lain awake
most of the night, how could it be otherwise? Yet how
could she sleep with her brain in a whirl?

Over and over again she had asked herself how Sir
Arthur Hix ever came to write such a lovely poem.
The question that followed was equally unanswerable:
How had he come to write letters of such sincerity
that her cousin's heart had been completely won over?

Last week, when she had asked Mr. Quartermaine
about Sir Arthur, the publisher had referred to the
baronet's work as uninspired and derivative. "His subject matter is trite, and his rhymes are as commonplace as a schoolboy's." Then he had informed her
that if she suspected that Sir Arthur was the man who
corresponded with her cousin, she was wrong.

She had not suspected it, not for a moment, but
what if Mr. Phineas Quartermaine was wrong? Why
would Sir Arthur lie about having written "The Blue
Campion"? It would seem a very foolish thing to do,
especially right there in front of members of his own
poetry society—men who would know if what he said
was the truth or a fabrication.

Olivia's emotions swirled around and around, as if
caught in an eddy, and certain she could not survive
another day without at least trying to discover the

truth, she decided to go immediately to Holburn Street to see the publisher.

"You must go now?" Esme asked. "You cannot be serious. Surely this business of getting Jane's poems published can wait one day."

"No, it cannot."

"But, Livvy, where are your priorities? We are invited to take tea with Lady White! A duke's daughter-in-law!"

"Since the invitation is for four o'clock, and it is now only half past nine, I see no reason to be concerned. I doubt I shall need all seven of those hours just to dress for tea."

"But she is a marchioness!"

Rightly determining that further argument would accomplish nothing, Olivia gave Esme a hug, promised to return with time to spare, then went to her bed-chamber. Once there, she donned her yellow challis walking dress and her gold velvet spencer. It occurred to her as she tied the gold ribbons of her chip straw bonnet that this was the same ensemble she had worn when she rode in Hyde Park with David Crighton, only this time she had dispensed with the silk veil.

Recalling how David had teased her about wanting to kiss her, and how very much she had wanted to have him take her in his arms and kiss her as she had dreamed of being kissed, she felt a stab of regret as painful as any knife wound. Even if she found solid proof that he was not the man Cousin Jane loved, it was possible Olivia had already ruined any chance *she* might have of winning David Crighton's heart.

Their drive to Richmond in his curricle had been even more wonderful than the drive to Hyde Park, with David teasing her and flirting with her in such a way that she was certain his intentions toward her were serious. She had no doubt that he felt that same almost pre-destined attraction to her that she felt for him. After the final leg of the journey, however, when

Miss Agnes Averill was his passenger, he seemed changed, almost as if he were angry with Olivia. She had tried to remember if she had done or said anything to give him a dislike of her, but she could recall nothing.

Then, of course, she had learned that he was known as "The Bard of Eton." After that, the entire day had turned into the sort of nightmare one hoped never to relive. "So do not relive it," she told herself.

There was a bit of wisdom she had learned in school, warning against borrowing the next day's troubles, something about the evils of each day being sufficient to worry about on that day. Trying to recall the quotation, she was so deep in thought that she had descended the staircase and crossed the hotel lobby without being aware of her surroundings. It was only when she reached the entrance door, which a footman hurried to hold open for her, that she looked around her, quite surprised to discover that she had come this far.

If she had been paying attention, she would not have collided with the broad-shouldered man who was entering from Albemarle Street. But she was not attending, and the impact of bumping into that hard, muscular frame was not unlike that of running headlong into a stone wall. "Oh! Forgive me, sir."

His strong hands grasped her upper arms, to keep her from falling, and as she looked up into those familiar dark blue eyes, he said her name, his voice soft and appealingly low. "It is I who should ask your pardon. At least twice over."

David! He was the last person she had expected to see, and unprepared for the encounter, she was shocked anew at the pure animal magnetism that flowed from this man to her. For a moment, she felt as if there was no air to breathe, and she was obliged to gulp twice before she could speak. "Lord Crighton. Why are you here?"

"I have come to see you, Miss Mallory. Please, I see two empty chairs just over there. May we sit down for a few minutes?"

There was nothing Olivia wanted to do more than to talk with David Crighton, but she was already at her wit's end over this matter of Sir Arthur, and she wondered if now was the right time to add further fuel to the fire inside her brain. "Can this not wait for another day, my lord?"

"No. It has already waited far too long."

"But I was on my way out. To Holburn Street, on a matter of business."

"I know the way to Holburn Street, and my curricle is just outside. May I drive you to your destination? I do so need to speak with you."

"About what?"

Taking her simple question as permission, he took her arm and led her to the curricle. After helping her aboard, he tossed a coin to the footman who stood at the horses' heads, then took the reins in his hands. "Which end of Holburn, Miss Mallory?"

"Near Leather Lane. Number eleven. It is the home of Quartermaine Publishing."

He looked at her for several seconds, a question she could not read in his eyes, then he gave the chestnuts the office to be on their way. After driving for a number of blocks in total silence, he said, "So, it is true. You are a poet."

"I? No, of course not. I have no talent for rhyming. I told you that the other day."

"So you did," he said very quietly. "And I believed you. Unfortunately, Miss Averill informed me, quite without realizing that she was contradicting your word, that you had a book of poems you wished to see published."

It was Olivia's turn to stare. He thought she had lied to him. "And is that why you behaved in that very odd manner at the alfresco breakfast?"

"My behavior was not odd, madam, it was unforgivably boorish. A circumstance for which I hope you will allow me to apologize. I let my anger and my disappointment rule my better judgment, and the only possible excuse I can offer is that I was concerned for my uncle."

Though Olivia failed to see what his concern for his uncle had to do with being angry with her, she was more than willing to forgive him for acting badly. After all, there was something she desperately needed to know about him. And what better time than the present to ask. "Lieutenant Windham referred to you as 'The Bard of Eton.' I wonder, my lord, why you never mentioned your own poetic talent."

Though it was difficult to discern beneath his tan, Olivia could have sworn the gentleman blushed. "The sobriquet was not given to me because I possess any degree of talent, Miss Mallory. I got it because in my youth I penned a limerick about my Latin professor, a taskmaster without an iota of humor."

"A limerick?"

"A particularly crude one, I fear, which made it all the more popular with very young boys."

Olivia knew very little about schoolboys, but if David said the limerick was crude, she was willing to take his word for it.

"Naturally," he continued, "the deuced thing made the rounds of the school, and even some of the upper level boys congratulated me. For a lad of ten, this was high praise indeed, and I began to think of myself as a clever fellow. Until, of course, the limerick found its way into the headmaster's morning post. Needless to say, my 'talent,' as you called it, earned me a caning that obliged me to stand for the entire week that followed."

Though a caning was no laughing matter, Olivia could not contain her amusement, and when she laughed, so did he. "Did anyone ever tell you, Miss Mallory, that you are a heartless woman?"

Olivia was so happy to have that "Bard of Eton" matter cleared up that she would not allow herself to postpone discovering the most important fact: Did he know Jane Frant? Without giving herself time to think, she said, "The poems I wish to see published were written by my cousin."

"Your cousin?"

She took a deep breath before continuing. "Her name was Jane Frant."

When Lord Crighton did not so much as bat an eye, Olivia felt as if her heart began to beat again after a long period of inactivity. Unable to stop herself, she smiled. When he returned her smile, it was as if the sun had reappeared after a month-long seclusion and was shining on her alone. "Jane Frant," she repeated. "You never heard of my cousin, my lord?"

"No," he replied, his voice totally without guile, "but when her poems are published, I promise to be the first in line to purchase a copy of the book."

"No need, sir, I will send you a copy."

They had turned onto Holburn, and as he pulled the chestnuts to the curb, he leaned very close to Olivia, his words almost loverlike. "Better still," he said, "I will come to you, wherever you are, so that you may place the book directly into my hands."

Wherever you are. Olivia could not believe how happy those words made her, and too bemused to remember that she had not asked him her final question, she allowed him to hand her down from the curricle. It was only later, after Mr. Phineas Quartermaine had delivered the blow that threatened to break her heart, that she remembered she had failed to ask Lord Crighton the reason for his dislike of Sir Arthur Hix.

"Miss Mallory," the publisher said, greeting her almost as an old friend, "what can I do for you?"

Coming directly to the point, she said, "I heard a poem yesterday, a short but rather pretty piece that

Sir Arthur Hix claims to have written. I wondered if you could tell me if it was true."

The large gentleman placed his hands on his desk, looking at his splayed fingers rather than at his visitor. "Personally, madam, I doubt the man has ever written anything that could be called pretty, but I suppose there could always be a first time. Can you recite a few lines of the piece? Or have you a copy of it with you?"

She had brought the much-folded copy from Cousin Jane's diary, but for some reason she was loath to expose it to curious eyes. "The poem is called 'The Blue Campion,' and it speaks of the flowers growing on a gray stone wall, and the poet passing them by."

The publisher studied his fingers for a moment longer, then nodded. "I know that poem. It is one of Crighton's. From his last book, I believe."

Crighton's! From his *last* book!

Olivia thought she might faint, though this time the cause was not tainted fish but the emotional sullying she felt from having believed David's lies. She had convinced herself that what she saw reflected in those dark blue eyes was tender feelings for her. Tender feelings? Ha! He had lied to her twice, and he had done so with a smile so beguiling that when she saw it, she could think of nothing else.

What a fool she was! He lied to her, and she believed him. She believed him because she wanted to believe him. It was that simple.

David Crighton was not only a published poet, but one whose work was recognized by people in the business. Furthermore, he claimed he had never heard of Jane Frant. That lying cad!

Grasping the last remaining bit of her sanity, and holding to it with all her strength, she asked Mr. Quartermaine why Sir Arthur would lay claim to a poem he did not write.

"Hix hates Crighton," he said. "Last year, when Crighton's newest book came out, Sir Arthur went all over town claiming that a number of the poems in the collection had been plagiarized, that they had been written by him years earlier, when he was in school. I believe he even threatened to sue. Naturally, nothing ever came of the threat, and for the most part, no one who knew the baronet believed his accusations."

That explained why Lord Crighton disliked Sir Arthur. It did not, however, explain why he had lied to Olivia once again. He had lied about the poetry, and he had lied about knowing Jane Frant. Poor Cousin Jane. It would have broken her heart if she had suspected that the man she loved would one day deny knowing her.

Olivia made short work of leaving the publisher's office, and once outside the Holburn Street building, she hailed a passing hackney, comforted by the thought that she would soon be hidden from view inside the dimness of the public carriage. "Grillon's Hotel, please."

The one bright spot left in her world had been the knowledge that David Crighton would not be waiting for her outside the publishing house. She had told him not to remain, for she had no idea how long she would be. Thankfully, he had acquiesced, for she only just managed to keep the tears from spilling down her face in the publisher's presence. There was no way she could have controlled them in front of David. Not after what she had learned about that so-called gentleman.

Liars. Deceivers of all types. Men who claimed ownership of things they did not own. Men who professed their innocence while hiding their guilt. Olivia wished she had never come to London.

In truth, she wished she had never found her cousin's poems and formed the idea of seeing them published. It was all a mistake, and the mistake was hers and hers alone. What made her think that a person as private as Jane Frant would want the world reading her poetry? As for allowing any of her correspondence to be printed, Jane would have been mortified by the very idea. As for Olivia, she would be mortified if anyone ever found out that she had given her heart to the same blackguard who had made a fool of her cousin.

Thankfully, there was still time to correct her mistake regarding the publication of the poems. As soon as she got back to the hotel, Olivia would write a letter to Mr. Quartermaine, explaining to the editor that she had changed her mind about the book. She would ask him to return the copies Esme had written out so neatly, for she was officially withdrawing her permission to print Jane Frant's poems. And under no circumstances would she ever agree to a publishing of even one line of the lady's correspondence.

Once the letter was written, Olivia would inform Esme and Hepzebah that they were returning to Suffolk as soon as travel arrangements could be made. They would not wait for their own coach and driver to be summoned; instead, Olivia would hire a post chaise and a postilion. Even the slowest "yellow boy" would travel faster than their antiquated Berlin, and now that she had made up her mind to leave, speed was important to Olivia.

Hepzebah would be pleased to be returning earlier than planned, but Esme would not. Esme had enjoyed her introduction to London, and she would not relish returning to St. Guilford one hour before the promised fortnight was over. There were still sights she had not seen. Things she had not done, and—

Lady White's tea! Olivia groaned. The invitation from the marchioness had completely slipped her mind, but she would wager twenty years of her life that Esme had not forgotten. Her sister would never agree to send around a note of regret, not to a duke's daughter-in-law. Yet how could Olivia sit in a stranger's withdrawing room, making small talk, when her heart was broken, and when every bit of faith she had ever had in the male population had been destroyed?

All she wanted to do was throw herself facedown on her bed and cry until there were no tears left, then sleep until she could wake without ever again thinking of David Crighton. Because she knew that neither of those things was likely to happen, she resigned herself to the fact that she could not escape the afternoon's socializing. She would have to pretend that all was well, at least until after the marchioness's tea.

Once that trial was endured, Olivia would face the even more difficult task of convincing Esme that they must return home immediately.

Her sister knew nothing of Jane Frant's letters. Nor had she the least inkling that their quiet, dutiful spinster cousin had kept a diary, one containing page after page of her most intimate thoughts, including the fact that she had been in love. It would be necessary to apprise Esme of both the letters and the diary. It might even be necessary to tell her sister about Lord Crighton's part in the entire affair, and how the older sister Esme looked up to for guidance had been as big a fool as Cousin Jane, believing every lying word that had passed David Crighton's lips.

The thought of his lips sent a shiver through Olivia, and she could contain her tears no longer. They spilled over at last, coursing down her face to fall upon the front of her gold spencer. She had wanted so to be kissed by him. She had wanted to feel his arms around her, and to experience the sensation of pressing her body against the length of his strong, muscular frame. She had dreamed of how it would be to have him draw her hard against him, then whisper that he loved her. Loved her so much that—

"Enough!" Tears continued to spill down her face, and after swiping at the salty liquid with the backs of her gloved hands, Olivia forced herself to forget those dreams of love that could never be. Instead, she concentrated on what she would do if Esme refused to accept the truth of Lord Crighton's involvement in this whole sordid story. What if she believed that Olivia was merely making it up to get her own way about returning to Suffolk? Deciding that she might need more tangible proof than her own and the publisher's word, Olivia knocked on the roof of the hackney.

"Yes, miss?"

"Take me to Hatchard's Bookstore, at one eighty-seven Piccadilly."

The jarvey mumbled something about females who never knew their own minds, but Olivia ignored him. She knew the exact proof she needed of David Crighton's duplicity, and if Hatchard's had a copy of David's latest book of poems, she meant to purchase it.

The instant the hackney stopped, Olivia jumped down to the pavement; then, after handing the jarvey three shillings and telling him to keep the change, she hurried through the bookstore entrance flanked by the small-paned bow windows. It being late morning, the famous emporium was filled to overflowing with book lovers and those who wished only to see and be seen, many of whom turned to stare at the unescorted woman who burst through the door like one demented.

Olivia ignored them all. She was here on a mission, and her resolve would not be weakened by the stares of the curious. Recalling that the poetry section was to the left, she did not pause at the polished oak information desk, but went directly to the bookshelf-lined walls.

The books and cantos were arranged alphabetically, starting on the highest shelf, and while Olivia ran her finger along the hundreds of cloth and leather spines, she mumbled to herself, "Ch. Cl. Co. Cr." There it was, the letters embossed in gold, "D. Crighton."

With trembling fingers, she removed the small

brown leather volume from the shelf. The title was *An English Wall*, and as she stared at the three words, her thoughts went to "The Blue Campion." Surely that poem was included in this little book.

Naturally, the pages were uncut, except for the title page and the copyright page, for the buyer expected to be the first to handle the inner pages. As Olivia opened the front cover and removed the thin, translucent sheet of paper that was placed there to protect the title page from smudgy fingers, she saw something that made her breath come in little audible sobs deep in her throat.

On the title page, the author's entire name was given, and there, for all to see, was the name Denholm Crighton. *Denholm!* Not David. The poet was his uncle Denholm.

"May I help you with that?" asked a clerk whose red face told Olivia plainly that he had heard her muffled sobs.

She had come into the store for no other purpose than to buy the book of poems, but now, like one hypnotized, she placed the leather volume into the young man's outstretched hand. "I . . . I will come another time," she said.

People were already staring at her, and now, with a fresh supply of tears flooding her eyes, albeit happy tears, the interested audience had begun to whisper behind their hands. Not wanting to make a complete spectacle of herself, Olivia turned and hurried from the bookstore.

Once outside on the pavement, she blinked away the tears that were so unlike the ones she had shed not twenty minutes earlier. She looked around her. Her emotions had been bounced back and forth like a child's rubber ball, and she was too dazed to remember whether to go left or right to reach Albemarle Street and Grillon's Hotel.

While she stood at the curb, undecided what to do,

she looked across the street, on the north side of Piccadilly, at the brick-fronted building known as The Albany. Almost as if she had conjured him up, there in the forecourt of the building stood David Crighton, a small valise in his hand. He had just stepped off the porch, and like Olivia, he stopped and stared, as if unable to believe that she was there.

Still feeling like one under the influence of some hypnotic force, she crossed the busy street and walked directly to David, as she had wanted to do the first time she ever saw him. When she reached him, she stopped so that mere inches separated them.

"Miss Mallory? Olivia? Good God! Tell me what has happened to upset you."

"I— Oh, David."

When words failed her, she did the one logical thing she had done since she arrived in London. She put her right hand against his cheek and looked deeply into his eyes. "Oh, David, I am so happy to see you. In fact, I do not think I could have waited another minute."

Recognizing an invitation when he heard one, and with his heart still beating erratically as a result of the risks she had taken crossing the busy street in that reckless manner, he did what he had wanted to do since the first day he saw her. He wrapped his arms around her and kissed her full on the lips.

Chapter Twelve

$\mathcal{D}$avid Crighton, the eighth Baron Crighton, had kissed his share of women—perhaps more than his fair share—and a flattering number of those women had even instigated the kisses. Until that moment, however, he had never kissed a lady on a public street in broad daylight. Nor had he ever responded so to a simple kiss. A salty, untutored kiss at that!

He had left her on Holburn Street less than an hour ago, and when he looked up and saw her standing in front of Hatchard's, looking for all the world as if she did not know where she was, he had thought he was imagining the whole. Then, when she began to cross the traffic-choked street, as though impervious to the danger, he had known a heart-stopping fear.

Somehow she made it safely across Piccadilly, and when she was close enough for him to see her tear-stained face, he knew something terrible had happened. Had she been injured? Accosted by some ruffian?

David had faced some of the craftiest, cruelest men France had ever produced, yet he had never before experienced such fear. He felt as if his insides were being twisted first one way, then the other by some supernatural force intent on punishing him for past crimes. "Miss Mallory? Olivia?" he said, aware of the unsteadiness of his voice. "Good God! Tell me what has happened to upset you."

Obviously unable to reply, she merely smiled at him, and as if by magic, his fears disappeared. Then she had touched his cheek and told him, with a catch in her voice, that she was happy to see him.

Unable to stop himself, he dropped his valise and pulled her into his arms, crushing her pliant, womanly body against his. In that instant, the entire world disappeared. There was no Piccadilly, no traffic, no curious passersby. There was only David and Olivia, alone in each other's arms, their lips tasting, teasing, giving, taking until David was nearly mindless with desire.

Finally, when reality and sanity shouted to him to remember where he was, he broke the kiss and gently removed Olivia's arms from around his neck. Still holding her wrists, he looked into her kiss-softened face. "Do not think for a moment that I did not enjoy that, because I did—more than I can say. But I must ask why you—"

He stopped mid-question, for his cravat had grown so tight it threatened to choke the life from him, and he was obliged to let go of one of her wrists so he could run his finger down behind the knot in the linen, in order to relieve the knot inside his throat. As for the other expanding portions of his anatomy, adjusting those would have to wait for a bit more privacy.

Deciding that he needed to remove Olivia from this very public stage, David reclaimed his valise, holding it in front of him, then took her by the arm and led her to his curricle, which one of the Albany grooms had brought around to the curb moments ago. "I will drop you off at Grillon's," he said, "then I must leave town for a day or so. I received a message from my estate manager in Kent, and there is a matter that needs my attention at Crighton Park."

"You are going to Kent?" The huskiness of her voice told its own story about the effect their kisses

had on her, and it was all David could do to refrain
from pulling her back into his arms for another taste
of her sweet lips.

"My home is in Wexham," he said.

"Wexham."

"Yes. It is the family's principal seat, though there
is a snug little estate in the north York Moors, not far
from the coastal town of Whitby."

"Whitby," she repeated.

It was clear to see that neither of them had enough
sense at the moment to carry on an intelligent conversation, so David suggested they wait until he returned
to discuss that kiss and what had prompted it.
"Though I strongly recommend that we find some
quiet, and very private place for the discussion."

"Yes," she said, looking up at him in a way that
sorely tested his resolve not to kiss her again, "a very
private place."

He still could not believe the events of the past
quarter hour. As often as he had dreamed of making
love to her—of taking her to his bed and seeing her
lying beside him, her lovely red-blond hair billowing
across the satin of the pillows—he had never expected
to kiss her in a place so public anyone might have
seen them.

From the first moment he saw her, nearly a fortnight
ago, he had wanted her. Even before he knew her
name, he had endured nights where he dreamed she
came to him in his room, slid beneath the covers, and
pressed her warm, silken body against his. Those
dreams had driven him wild, but not as wild as the
sweet reality of holding her close and feeling her re-
spond to his kiss as he had known she would. God
help him, she had responded as if they had been created for each other.

Oddly enough, when he had asked the one question
he could not postpone—why she had allowed him to
kiss her at just that moment, and in such a public

place—the only answer she offered was, "Because I am so glad you are not a poet."

"But I told you that earlier, when we drove to Holburn Street. Why did you not kiss me then?"

"That," she said, "is a long and very involved story, and unless you wish to see me turn into a complete watering pot, you will allow me to postpone the telling of it until another day."

The drive to Grillon's was accomplished in a matter of minutes. Since David was absolutely certain it would be an egregious mistake for him to get out of the curricle in his present condition, he remained in place and merely handed Olivia down to the pavement. Neither of them offered a word of good-bye, and after tipping his hat, he waited only until she had passed through the hotel entrance before he drove away.

While he tooled the chestnuts through the busy London streets, headed southeastward toward the Lambeth horse ferry that would take him across the Thames and to the road that led to Wexham and Crighton Park, all David could think of was Olivia Mallory. The blood still ran hot through his veins, and though he knew without a doubt what he wanted to do that very minute, which was turn the curricle around, find Olivia, and carry her to the nearest bed, he knew that anything of that nature would have to wait.

What he needed to figure out now was where they went from here? He liked being with her—that went without saying—and he enjoyed talking with her, for she was as intelligent and spirited as she was beautiful. She was fun as well, and when he teased her, just watching her slow, appreciative smile did strange things to his heart. He could not remember a time when he had not wanted to touch her, and when he finally had been given the opportunity, the passion

that had taken fire between them had been unbeliev-
able. In fact, the entire experience had felt right, almost preordained.

He wanted her, he always had, but Olivia Mallory
was the marrying kind. The question he had to ask
himself: Was he?

The Hanover Square town house of the Marquis of
Pembury was quite handsome, though not nearly as
imposing as Olivia had expected. Naturally, with his
father, the Duke of Thornborough, still occupying the
older, far grander place around the corner from Burlington House, one assumed the marquis's present
abode was temporary, until such time as the present
duke went to his heavenly reward.

From the outside, the house was not much different
from its neighbors, but inside the architecture and the
elaborate interior set it apart. The octagonal vestibule
was decorated on all eight walls with canvases at least
fifteen feet tall and six feet wide. Olivia was not certain who had painted the pastoral scenes depicted on
those canvases, but there was no question that the
artist was a master.

"Ooh," Esme whispered when the very superior
butler led them up the handsome staircase that gave
access to the public rooms. "Is it not beautiful? Have
you ever seen anything so elegant?"

Olivia had, of course. She remembered their old
home, Mallory Manor, which had been inherited by a
distant male relative, as being quite nice. As well, during the three weeks of her come-out—before it was
cut short by the boating accident that claimed the lives
of her parents—Olivia had visited in the homes of
several of the other young ladies experiencing their
first seasons in society. Those homes, unlike Frant
House, Uncle Raeford's austere home in Suffolk, had
been decorated in the first style of elegance.

At the thought of meeting the marchioness, Esme,

as befit a young lady of her tender years, was a mass of nerves. Olivia, on the other hand, was calm almost to the point of sleepwalking. Discovering that David Crighton was not the poet who had captured her cousin's heart had been of such paramount importance to her that everything else seemed inconsequential. Everything, that is, except the kisses they had exchanged, and the marvelous emotional cocoon those kisses had spun around her.

The butler, after scratching discreetly at a raised-panel door trimmed in gold leaf, stepped inside the elegant blue and gold salon and announced the visitors. "My lady," he said, "Miss Mallory and Miss Esme Mallory."

To Olivia's surprise, a little squab of a woman, middle-aged, with graying brown hair and pince-nez spectacles, came forward, her lace-mittened hand extended politely. "Miss Mallory. Miss Esme. How kind of you to come."

The sisters sank into deep curtsies, then they each touched the two fingers offered them by their hostess.

If the marchioness was not particularly personable, neither was she more starched up than one might expect from a duke's daughter-in-law. After introducing the sisters to her other guests, Mrs. Gerard and Mrs. Beardsley-Brown, two matrons of a similar age as their hostess, she invited the young ladies to be seated. "My father-in-law means to join us presently," she said. "My brother, Lord Vere, was to address the House of Lords this afternoon, and his grace and the marquis went to offer him their support."

Almost immediately, the butler reappeared, followed by a liveried footman and two maids in crisp, white aprons and mob caps. A rosewood teapoy was set beside her ladyship's chair, so that she might dispense tea to her guests. As well, two occasional tables were drawn up to accommodate the two ornate silver platters that were filled almost to overflowing with plates of small delicacies, some of the treats forced into such odd shapes and tinted such unusual colors that they were unidentifiable to the Mallory sisters.

Olivia, still so love-smitten that she noticed very little, finally became aware that the two other guests were talking to each other behind their fans, while casting surreptitious glances in her direction.

"Miss Esme," Lady White said, once the delicate gold-handled Sevres teacups were passed around, "are you enjoying your visit to the city? I understand you have not been here previously."

"No, ma'am, this is my first visit, but I have enjoyed it prodigiously."

"And are you to be presented to Her Majesty?"

"No, ma'am. My sister and I came to town on a matter of business, not to partake of the season."

For some reason, the two guests, neither of whom had done more than nod to the sisters, both giggled like girls a third their age. "And what of you?" Mrs. Gerard asked Olivia. "Are you enjoying your stay 'prodigiously' as well?"

Something in the woman's tone—a slyness—put Olivia on the alert. "I am sure I do not know what you mean, ma'am. Is there any reason why I should not be enjoying it?"

Olivia had spoken more harshly than she would ordinarily have done, but she mistrusted the look in the eyes of Mrs. Beardsley-Brown, who had not yet said a word to anyone other than her friend. Uncle Raeford had once owned a dog that would occasionally sneak up on an unsuspecting chicken and grab it by the neck, shaking it until the poor fowl was as good as dead. The canine did not eat the bird, he merely slew it for the enjoyment of the kill, then left the poor creature jerking and twisting in the dirt. Mrs. Beardsley-Brown put Olivia in mind of that dog.

"I was at Hatchard's earlier," the woman said. "I believe I saw you there as well."

"Yes, ma'am. I was there."

The woman began to fan herself as if overheated, though it was obvious from the smile she could not hide that she was enjoying *herself* prodigiously. "Though it pains me to relate this, Hermione," she said, turning to Lady White, "I feel I must. Especially since you were so good as to inform us that you were previously unacquainted with these young persons."

Persons!

One of the mob-capped maids gasped, obviously shocked to hear a young lady referred to as a "person."

The marchioness set her pince-nez spectacles on her nose, the better to see the gossipy speaker. "What are you saying?"

"Just this," she replied, "that I saw that one—Miss Mallory, as she calls herself—behaving like the veriest strumpet."

"What!" Esme rose abruptly, unmindful of the hot, fragrant liquid she spilled down the front of her pretty pink silk frock. More than ready to defend her sister against her accuser, she said, "How dare you say such a vile thing about—"

"Hush, Esme." Olivia kept her voice as calm as possible under the circumstances. "Please take your seat, for her ladyship's guest has something to say, and I am persuaded she is not yet finished."

Mrs. Beardsley-Brown ignored her. "Miss Mallory entered the bookstore quite alone, Hermione, then after causing a stir of sorts in the store, she ran across the street to the Albany, where she positively flung herself at a gentleman, kissing him most wantonly. Naturally, the gentleman, who is a peer of somewhat dubious reputation, did nothing to dissuade her disgraceful behavior but returned her embrace. Finally, as if that were not enough, she climbed aboard the gentleman's curricle, still unescorted, mind you, and the two of them drove away."

"It is a lie!" Esme said, tears of anger spilling from her pretty green eyes. "My sister would not do anything like that."

"Miss Mallory," the marchioness said, "this is most shocking news, and I do not know what his grace will say when he hears it. Have you some explanation for your behavior?"

"Why, no, ma'am, I have not. At least, none I wish to share. I am a woman full grown, and there is no reason, familial or otherwise, why I need make you or your 'friends' privy to my thoughts or actions."

"What impertinence!" Mrs. Beardsley-Brown said. "Do you realize, young woman, that you are speaking to a marchioness?"

Olivia stood and set the lovely Sevres cup on one of the trays, then she took the cup from her sister's trembling hand and set it on the tray as well. "Come, Esme, we must be leaving, for I fear I have developed a headache."

Olivia took the linen napkin she still held and wiped away her sister's tears. "Do not distress yourself, my love."

"But, Livvy, why would that lady say such vicious things about you?"

"For the joy it brought her. And just to set the record straight, she is no lady, she is a chicken-killing bitch."

Olivia heard the woman's outraged gasp, but she did not look back. She merely linked her arm through her sister's, and the two of them exited the room. They went directly down the stairs, leaving a battery of gaping-mouthed servants in their wake, then continued through the entrance door, not stopping until they were once again on the pavement.

Rather than wait for a passing hackney, Olivia suggested they walk back to the hotel. "For never in my life have I needed fresh air more."

Being country bred, the young ladies had no trouble

whatsoever walking from Hanover Square to Grillon's,
and while they walked, Olivia apologized to her sister.
"You had so looked forward to this afternoon, and I
ruined it for you."

"Livvy, for heaven's sake, do not be a goose!"

"But it is true. This might have been the connection
you needed, for if the marchioness chose to take you
under her wing, you might have had a proper season.
Maybe even a voucher for Almack's."

"Bah! As if I wanted that."

"I wanted it for you, my love, and I hope you know
that I would never willingly embarrass you in that
manner."

"Me! But, Livvy, what of the embarrassment to
you? What of all those horrible things that spiteful
she-cat said about you? Those malicious lies she
invented?"

"Malicious she certainly was, but almost everything
she said was true."

Surprised by the admission, Esme stopped walking
and turned to look directly at her sister. "You . . . you
actually threw yourself at some man and kissed him?"

"I said, 'almost everything' was true."

Esme's mouth fell open. "But who? Why?"

"The 'why' can wait until we are in the privacy of
our suite. So much has happened since we came to
town, and I had meant to tell you everything later
anyway. For now, I will say only that it had to do with
Cousin Jane's poems."

Always a clever girl, Esme said, "Must I wait for
the 'who' as well?"

Olivia shook her head. "It was David Crighton."

Apparently not as surprised as Olivia thought she
would be, Esme said, "You kissed Lord Crighton? In
a public place, where others could see you?"

"I did. In fact, it was not too unlike what that dread-
ful woman said, for by my actions I gave him every

reason to believe he might take me in his arms and kiss me."

Her angry tears suddenly a memory, the young girl laughed. "Livvy, if that is not just like you. But tell me instantly, did you enjoy it? The kiss, I mean."

"It was wonderful," Olivia said. "And to quote a certain she-cat, I enjoyed it prodigiously!"

Chapter Thirteen

"*I* hope I may not have ruined your chances with Lieutenant Windham?"

"Joel?" Esme seemed surprised. "What a foolish notion, Livvy."

"Is it?"

Though Esme protested that she and the lieutenant were merely friends, and that she had not formed a *tendre* for him, Olivia began to suspect the young lady, like Mr. Shakespeare's heroine, "protested too much."

The sisters had partaken of an early dinner, after which Olivia had gone to her bedchamber where she wrote three letters. She held those letters in her hand now, for she had sent Hepzebah down to the lobby to fetch a footman willing to deliver them right away.

One letter was to Kitty Selby, thanking her for her friendship, and explaining what had occurred at the marchioness's tea. Convinced that her name would be all over town by tomorrow, Olivia had informed Kitty that if she felt it necessary to disclaim any knowledge of the Mallory sisters, that they would understand.

The second letter was for Denholm Crighton. The message was short and to the point, requesting a half hour of his time at noon the next day, and informing him that she wished to return something that belonged to him. The third letter was to Mr. Phineas Quartermaine, advising him of her decision not to have

Jane Frant's poems published, and asking for the return as soon as possible of the copies he held.

The next day, though Olivia had received no reply to her letter to Denholm Crighton, she made good her promise to call upon him at his town house in Grosvenor Square. A tall, ebony case clock near the foot of the staircase was sounding the noon hour at the very moment the footman admitted her to the town house. A truly odd-looking fellow, the servant looked more like a Bow Street Runner than a footman in a gentleman's establishment, and from the way he looked Olivia up and down, she could well imagine that he was weighing the advisability of searching her for weapons.

What a very strange sort of house, to be sure!

"Mrs. Crighton is away from home at the moment, miss."

"Thank you for that information, but I have come to see Mr. Denholm Crighton. You may inform your employer that Miss Mallory has come on a matter of business. I sent him a letter last evening, so I imagine he will be expecting me."

"As you say, miss. If you will be so good as to wait here, I will see if Mr. Crighton is available."

The servant motioned toward a straight-backed chair whose polished ebony matched that of the case clock and a small console table, and though Olivia seated herself on the edge of the uncomfortable chair, she had only a minute to wait before the footman returned.

"Mr. Crighton will see you, miss. Follow me to the bookroom, if you please."

"I bid you good day, Miss Mallory," Denholm Crighton said, rising from a handsome, mahogany knee-hole desk. The gentleman's complexion looked quite pale, and he seemed to have aged a year since Olivia saw him last.

After a brief curtsy, she thanked him for agreeing to see her.

"Not at all. Though I must confess to being quite at a loss as to the reason for your visit."

When she would have spoken, he interrupted her long enough to ask if he might offer her some refreshment.

"I thank you, sir, but this is not a social call."

The footman, unabashedly curious, remained by the door until his employer bid him take himself away. The moment the door closed behind the fellow, Denholm Crighton motioned Olivia to one of two wing chairs flanking the fireplace in the handsomely paneled room. Once she was seated, he took the chair opposite.

"Now, Miss Mallory, how may I help you? Your letter, which I must tell you took me quite by surprise, mentioned that you wished to return something that belongs to me. Quite frankly, I cannot recall a single possession of mine that has gone missing."

"Perhaps it will aid your memory, sir, if I begin by telling you that I am from Suffolk. From the village of St. Guilford, to be exact."

Moments ago, Denholm Crighton had appeared pale, now he looked positively ashen. "St. Guilford," he said. The words sounded hollow, as though they came from some deep, empty place, and Olivia knew that this time she had not made a mistake. Denholm Crighton was definitely the man who had written the poems and letters to her cousin.

"I live at Frant House," she continued, "and along with my sister, I am the heiress to everything that once belonged to my uncle, Mr. Raeford Frant, and to his daughter, my cousin, Miss Jane Frant."

At the mention of Jane's name, Denholm Crighton hid his face in his hands, his long, tapered fingers mussing his graying hair. Clearly he was upset, but if he cried or merely hid his face, Olivia could not tell.

After a time, he leaned his head back against the high back of the chair, his eyes closed. "Did . . . did she suffer?" he asked at last.

This was not the question Olivia expected. "No," she replied, "I do not believe so. My cousin slipped away quietly."

The ragged sigh seemed torn from him. After a time, he said, "My last letter to Jane, which was sent some time in November, was returned to me by Mrs. Blair, the seamstress who acted as our go-between. In Mrs. Blair's rather brief missive, she said only that Jane and her father had both succumbed to virulent cases of influenza."

That last, dreaded word had no sooner passed his lips than Olivia saw tears slip from beneath his closed eyelids to slide unheeded down his rather gaunt face.

Though she did not wish to feel sympathy for this man, Olivia's heart would not obey her wishes. He might be married to another, but it was obvious that he had loved her cousin. "Jane was weak from nursing her father, so when she became ill, she had no strength left in her to fight. She went very quickly."

For a time, nothing more was said, and the only sound in the room was the gentleman's rather ragged breathing. "I knew Jane only through her words," he said, "but I have never loved anyone as I loved her. She looked upon my very soul, just as I looked upon hers."

Surprising Olivia, Denholm Crighton leaned forward, his elbows upon his thin knees and his face once again hidden in his hands. A single sob was torn from him, and the sound was so forlorn, so lonely, that Olivia was obliged to admit that the man's feelings for Jane were genuine.

"Heaven help me," he said, "for the kindest, dearest person I ever knew is gone, and I must remain in a world without her—a world deprived of sunlight and stars, without even the promise of joy."

There could be no doubt of his sincerity, and Olivia experienced the same discomfort she had felt when reading her cousin's diary. To stem any further confidences, she told him why she had come to town.

When she mentioned a possible book of Jane's poems, he looked up, the ghost of a smile on his quivering lips. "A book of her poems? I would love that," he said, "even though I cannot convince myself that Jane would have liked it. You, of all people, must know what a private person she was."

So, he knew Jane well enough to know that.

"Actually," Olivia said, "the publisher appreciated Jane's poems, but he felt he could not make a success of a book containing her work alone."

"Then I do not understand, Miss Mallory."

"Neither did I at first. What the publisher wanted was Jane's poems interspersed by those poems you had sent her. As well, he wanted samples of the correspondence that passed between the two of you."

Denholm Crighton stared at her, and though his eyes were still damp with tears, the blue orbs had grown cold as a mountain lake. When he spoke, there was an edge to his voice. "I see," he said. "So you have come to my home today not to discuss one whose memory should be sacrosanct. Instead, you have come in hopes of procuring written permission from me so that this so-called publisher can put together some sort of rubbish posing as literature."

"Actually, sir, my reason for coming was to—"

"Say no more, if you please, Miss Mallory, for I want no part of your scheme. I am well acquainted with the sort of book it would be, and I assure you it would have nothing to do with the presentation of true poetry. Such books are filled with salacious trash, and their only purpose is to titillate the minds of those jaded hedonists who flock to London every spring in search of scandal to relieve their constant ennui."

He swore beneath his breath. "I suppose the publisher offered you a great deal of money."

Olivia did not dignify that accusation with a response. Instead, she reached into her reticule and removed every copy of Denholm Crighton's poems, plus every letter written in his hand. "These are yours," she said. "I believe my cousin would wish me to return them to you."

He merely stared at the small stack of vellum, which Jane Frant had tied with a pretty yellow ribbon. When he did not offer to take the stack from her, Olivia placed it on a side table. Her task completed, she rose from the wing chair. "And now, Mr. Crighton, I will bid you good day."

The man her cousin had loved remained in the chair beside the fireplace, as if unable to move, weighted down by the pain of his memories. Olivia did not attempt to reclaim his attention. Instead, she let herself out of the bookroom, closing the door softly behind her, then leaning against it for support.

She had known the meeting would not be pleasant, but she had not reckoned on coming away with such mixed feelings about Denholm Crighton. On the one hand, the man's insulting assumptions about her motives had made her unbelievably angry. On the other hand, she had experienced a heart-wrenching sympathy for a man who had lost the woman he loved.

But was that sympathy merited? After all, he was a married man, and though he and Jane Frant never met physically, there were those who would say that the spiritual and emotional bond the two poets had shared was a form of adultery. Perhaps the most egregious form.

And yet, who was Olivia to sit in judgment of others? She had made enough mistakes this past fortnight to satisfy her lifetime's quota, and she wanted no part of throwing stones at two people whose only sin was in loving each other.

She no longer doubted that Denholm loved her cousin every bit as much as Jane loved him. Truth to tell, if Olivia was any judge of the matter, the gentleman was grieving still, which would account for the appearance he gave of sleepwalking through life.

Hindsight being so much clearer than foresight, Olivia could see now that she should never have become involved in this entire affair. She was not sorry she had found her cousin's poems, but considering everything that had followed her visit to Mr. Phineas Quartermaine, she regretted most sincerely having tried to get the poetry published. Certainly she wished she had not read Jane's diary, and above all else, she wished she had never come to see Denholm Crighton.

Eager to escape this house, with its air of sadness, Olivia pushed away from the bookroom door. Only then did she realize that she was not alone in the vestibule. Augusta Crighton stood quite near the entrance door, having just returned from some errand or other, and if heightened color and eyes filled with passion were any indication, Denholm's wife was livid.

"You!" she all but screamed. "How dare you show your face in my house!"

Taken by surprise, Olivia said, "Forgive me, ma'am, if my coming here was not convenient for you, but my business was with your husband. There was a matter that needed to be—"

"Stop! Say no more, Miss Mallory, for I have no wish to hear anything that comes from your lips."

Augusta crossed the foyer in a few agitated steps, leaving the footman standing in the open doorway, his mouth agape. She stopped just in front of Olivia, and though they were close enough to speak in quiet tones, Denholm Crighton's wife did not lower her voice. "You must know that your name is now a byword among the *ton*. It is all over town how you insulted Lady White's guests yesterday, after disgracing yourself in public with my nephew."

It had all but slipped Olivia's mind that David was the nephew of Denholm and Augusta Crighton, for he was so unlike the middle-aged couple. Even so, Olivia offered no explanation for her behavior of the previous day.

Augusta laughed, but the sound was totally devoid of humor. "Do you think my nephew will marry you? He will not! David knows full well the sort of female he must take for his wife. Like all the Crighton men, he is proud of his lineage and totally cognizant of what is due his family name. He will do what is expected of the eighth Baron Crighton. When David marries, it will be to a *lady*, one of excellent family and impeccable reputation."

Mortified to be spoken to in this manner, Olivia tried to find a way to stanch the woman's vitriolic outpouring. "Madam, you are mistaken if you believe that I—"

"Be advised, Miss Mallory, that my nephew bores easily. He will soon grow tired of you, and when he does, he will treat you as he treats all his mistresses. He will discard you with no more regard for your feelings than if you were a week-old newspaper."

"Madam! You go too far."

"Save your airs of injured virtue, young woman, and do not attempt to bamboozle me, for I am not as stupid as some people may wish to believe. Do you think I do not know who you are? I know you, Miss Mallory from St. Guilford! You are related to that Jezebel. That whore."

Having heard enough, Olivia tried to walk past the angry woman, but Augusta Crighton caught her by the wrist, her hold surprisingly strong for one so thin. "I am not the fool you and my husband take me for," she said, her voice husky with hatred.

Olivia attempted to pull away, to free her wrist, but without success. "I never thought you a fool, ma'am. If anything, I feel sympathy for—"

"I want none of your pity, you strumpet! You think I do not know why you are here, but I do. You wish to see what you can gain by showing yourself as my husband's ally, the only person who can possibly share in his bereavement. For all I know, you may be thinking that once my nephew throws you over, you can replace Jane Frant as my husband's paramour."

Olivia had been insulted yesterday at Lady White's, and again a few minutes ago by Denholm Crighton, but Augusta Crighton was more than insulting, she was spewing venom, and pure, raw hatred.

"Have you and that cousin of yours not done enough harm? She with her silly, inane poems?"

"How . . . how did you know about my cousin's poetry?"

"Do you think I did not read them? I read every nauseating line, as well as the letters the stupid whore sent my husband. *My* husband! *Mine!*" she screamed. "Until death do us part!"

Olivia stiffened. "Madam, I understand jealousy and anger, and as for making allowances for a wife's broken heart, I can do that as well. What I will not do is stand here and allow you to call my poor, gentle cousin by vile names she did nothing to deserve."

"Nothing to deserve!"

Augusta Crighton's face had gone poppy red, while her pale blue eyes contained the fire of madness. Before Olivia even suspected what the woman meant to do, Denholm's wife drew back her hand and slapped Olivia across the face, the blow so hard Olivia thought her jaw might be broken. She would have fallen to the floor had she not stepped back a pace and bumped against the straight-backed, polished ebony chair she had found so uncomfortable earlier.

Olivia had never been struck before, not even when she was a child, and not quite sure how to react, she held to the cold wood of the chair until she regained her balance. She had dropped her reticule, but at the moment that seemed unimportant. Thankfully, the very odd-looking footman had rushed to Augusta Crighton's side and taken her by the shoulders, forcibly restraining her from doing further damage.

"Madam," he said, "this will not do!"

Augusta tried to pull free of the man's hold. When she could not, she leaned around him where she could see Olivia. "Get out of my house!" she yelled. "And leave my husband alone."

More than glad to do both, Olivia stumbled to the heavy entrance door, grateful that it was still open. As she hurried down the front stairs to the pavement, she heard Augusta screaming at her, shouting some sort of threat about filing a lawsuit if there were any more dead cats.

Dead cats!

Since this insane pronouncement seemed just one more bit of proof that the woman was deranged, Olivia continued in her flight, not pausing until she was several blocks beyond Grosvenor Square. Gasping for breath, and still shaking badly, she held her hand to her injured cheek, quite certain that all five of Augusta Crighton's fingers were imprinted on her skin. People on both sides of the street stared at her as if she were a raree-show, and Olivia wished with all her heart that she had the veil she had worn that day she rode with David in Hyde Park.

At thoughts of David, a sob escaped Olivia's throat. How much of what Augusta Denholm said about her nephew was true? David's was an old and illustrious lineage, that much was indisputable, and it would not be in the least surprising if he was proud of his family name. But would he do what was expected of him by marrying a female whose family was equally illustrious?

Olivia was a gentleman's daughter, and the grand-daughter of a respected general. Furthermore, she was in possession of a substantial residence and a modest inheritance. Though most of society would consider her worthy of being the wife of the eighth Baron Crighton, there were many who would not. Especially not if her name had become a byword in the *ton*.

But would David care for that? Even more importantly, what would be his reaction when he discovered that his uncle had been in love with Olivia's cousin? Olivia wished she knew the answers to those questions.

In so many ways David was still a mystery to her. She knew that she loved him, and from the way he had returned her kiss yesterday, she had thought that he loved her as well. Unfortunately, she would not be the first female to delude herself where matters of the heart were concerned.

Yes, he had kissed her, kissed her with a passion that made her head spin and her heart sing, but did he envision her as his future wife? Or did he think of her more in the light of a prospective mistress?

Could it be that Augusta was in the right of it, linking Olivia with David's previous *chères amies*? Not surprisingly, Olivia found that possibility far more distressing than the pain in her cheek.

By the time she reached Grillon's, the throbbing in her jaw had subsided somewhat, as had the stinging of her skin, but still afraid that evidence of the blow remained, she held a handkerchief to her cheek. She made it through the hotel lobby and up the broad staircase with a few shreds of her dignity still intact, but by the time she arrived at the door to the suite, the tears would no longer be denied.

To her horror, the first person she saw when she entered the sitting room was Lieutenant Windham. He and Esme sat on the rose settee, their hands interlocked and their heads close together in quiet conversation. "Livvy!" Esme said, jumping up as though she had been caught doing something reprehensible. "I did not expect you so soon."

At the guileless remark, Esme's face turned the

color of the settee. "What I meant to say is, Joel came by to bring you a letter from Lady Selby. I had one, as well, and in mine Kitty said that you are a total widgeon if you think she cares about anything those odious friends of Lady White's might say or—" As if only just realizing that her sister was not her usual self, Esme took a tentative step toward her. "Livvy?"

Olivia still held the handkerchief to her cheek, but when she looked directly at her younger sister, her tear-ravaged face must have told its own story, for Esme gasped. "Oh, Livvy, you are hurt. What on earth has happened?"

Before Olivia could reply, Esme ran to her and threw her arms around her sister's waist. Olivia allowed the embrace, but in a matter of seconds, the would-be comforter's blond head was on her older sister's shoulder, and Esme was sobbing so loudly that Olivia was obliged to comfort her. "Shh. Hush now, Esme, there's a good girl. What has happened is now in the past, and I have come to no permanent harm."

"But, Livvy? You—"

"Shh," she whispered, her mouth close to her sister's ear. "We will discuss this later, when we are alone." In a louder voice, she said, "I shudder to think what Lieutenant Windham must be thinking of us. If I know anything of gentlemen, he will be wishing himself anyplace but trapped in a small room with two watering pots."

The military gentleman had been studying Olivia rather intently, and she was not surprised to see that his still youthfully handsome face had taken on the hard cast of a stone fence. When he spoke, his words, though softly uttered, were shored up with steel. "Miss Mallory, I beg you will tell me who dared lay a hand on you."

Olivia shook her head. "It is of no consequence, Lieutenant, for I am persuaded I shall be right as a trivet in—"

"It is of every consequence," he replied, "for as your future brother, I claim the right to thrash the blackguard within an inch of his life."

It was a testament to Olivia's common sense that she chose the least important of those two revelations to address first. "The person who struck me was not a man, so I fear your chivalrous offer, as much as I thank you for it, would be inappropriate in an officer and a gentleman. But more importantly, what is this about your being my future brother?"

Lieutenant Windham snapped to attention and made Olivia a formal bow. "We shall, of course, require your consent, Miss Mallory, since your sister has not yet reached her majority. But not half an hour ago, Esme made me the happiest of men by agreeing to become my wife."

Chapter Fourteen

"And that is just about all there is to tell," Esme said.

She settled herself on the foot of Olivia's bed, where the late afternoon sunshine coming through the small mullioned window created eight crosslike patterns on the counterpane. "Napoleon is finally headed for the island of Elba to begin his exile, and troops are needed to make certain he gets there without interference from either friend or foe. When Joel received word that he was to return to his regiment within a fortnight to form part of the escort detail, nothing would do but that he—Joel that is," she said with an accompanying giggle, "not the Emperor—must come to me immediately."

She sighed like one taking part in a beautiful dream. "Joel wants a Christmas wedding, with me dressed in white velvet and carrying a bouquet of roses festooned with holly and ivy. Is that not the most romantic thing you ever heard?"

"The most," Olivia replied quietly, pressing to her cheek the cloth her sister had just freshened in the basin of cold water Hepzebah had left on the bedside table. In truth, Olivia neither needed nor wanted the cold compresses, but she bore the ministrations for her sister's sake, for Esme had been most sincerely distressed at the thought of someone striking her older sister.

Esme meant well, but she was no nurse, and with her thoughts safely returned to the romance of her newly declared love and the future wedding plans, she had been careless in wringing out the alternating clothes. As a consequence, the bed pillows were damp, and there was a trail of water across the covers Olivia had pulled up to her shoulders in an attempt to fight off the chills that had her in their grip.

Though she genuinely wished she could share in her sister's joy at this unexpected betrothal, Olivia had difficulty ridding her mind of the very ugly scene that had taken place in Grosvenor Square. Thankfully, neither Esme nor Hepzebah had pressured Olivia for an account of what had happened to her, and for their forbearance she would be eternally grateful.

"Naturally," Esme continued, "Joel would have preferred not to put his luck to the test, as he put it, so early in our acquaintance, but he knew his feelings were irrevocably fixed on me. His one fear, he said, was that he would return to England only to find me engaged to another." She shook her head, as if unable to understand the foolishness of the male sex. "Is he not a silly boy? As though I would even consider an offer from another man when there was the least chance I might have Joel Windham."

There was much more along that same line, explaining the lieutenant's reasons for seeking Esme's hand in what must appear most undue haste, but Olivia heard little of the actual words. Since her younger sister appeared more than satisfied with the occasional nod, interspersed with a well-timed reply of "Yes, he is handsome . . . or intelligent . . . or brave"—whichever comment best suited the question—Olivia felt she was being as good an older sister as her depleted physical and emotional states would allow.

She was more grateful than she could say when Hepzebah Potter scratched at the bedchamber door to tell Esme that the tea tray had arrived. "You go on out to the sitting room to have your tea, Miss Esme, while everything is still hot. I'll sit here with Miss Livvy. I've brought her a nice cuppa," she said, indicating the pretty blue and gold cup and saucer from which emanated a most inviting fragrance, "and this small package, which was just delivered by special messenger."

"Here," Esme said, taking the package from beneath the maid's arm. "Shall I open it for you, Livvy?"

"Please do."

Instead of placing the package on the bed or the desk, Esme held it in one hand, while with her other hand she tugged at the string that secured the brown wrapping paper. Unfortunately, she discovered too late that the package was not as well tied as she had thought, for when the knot gave way, she lost her grip and the contents fluttered to the floor. Dozens of sheets of paper lay scattered about the carpet, and as Esme stared at the clutter, she realized what they were. "It is Cousin Jane's poems," she said. "The ones I copied for the publisher."

When she bent down to retrieve the poems, she found among them a wafered letter. "For you," she said, handing the missive to her sister.

Olivia felt certain she already knew the contents of the letter. Even so, she broke the wafer and read the few lines aloud.

Miss Mallory,

Enclosed are the poems you allowed me to consider for publication. I regret that we could not come to some mutually agreeable arrangement. Should you ever reconsider your decision, I am still interested. Naturally, the same stipulations would apply.

> *Until then, I remain, Yr. Obt. Serv.*
> *Phineas Quartermaine, Publisher*

"Well, that is that, then."

"Yes," Olivia agreed, "that does seem to be the end of the matter."

Esme gathered the last of the poems and stood, and once she had arranged the papers in a neat pile, she asked Olivia what she wished her to do with them. "Shall I take these copies to my bedchamber and put them in Mama's portable writing desk, along with the original poems?"

Recalling Jane Frant's diary, which still lay inside the little cherry Davenport desk, Olivia shook her head. "Just put the copies over there," she said, pointing to the green leather-covered top. "I will deal with them in the morning. For now, I think I should like to try for a bit of sleep."

Though it was early to be retiring for the night, Olivia wanted nothing so much as solitude and silence. She needed both to bring some sort of order to her jumbled thoughts. Though more tired than she could ever remember being, her fatigue came not so much from Augusta Crighton's physical blow, as from the mental blow the woman had dealt her with the suggestion that David would grow tired of Olivia, as he did with all his mistresses, then discard her like so much rubbish.

Esme set the poems on the desk, then kissed her fingers to her sister and quit the room. Meanwhile, the maid set the cup of tea on the bedside table, then removed from her apron pocket a small blue vial, which she held so Olivia could see it.

"Laudanum? No, Hepzebah, I do not want—"

"Now, before you refuse, Miss Livvy, let me have my say. I know you've never been one to quack yourself, and for the most part I agree with you. However, the way I see it, right now healing sleep's what you need, and if this'll help you get it, then I'm all for it." She took the top off the vial. "What say you to just a drop for the pain?"

Too exhausted to argue, Olivia nodded her consent, then watched as Hepzebah carefully added the single drop to the contents of the cup. "Now drink it all, Miss Livvy. No point in doing a thing halfway."

An obedient patient, Olivia drank every ounce of the fragrant tea, then handed the cup and saucer back to Hepzebah, who had moved the night candle to within easy reach. "There's a fresh candle here on the bedside table, Miss Livvy, in case you should wake in the night and want to get up, and if you've need of me, you know you have only to call my name."

"I know. Thank you, Hepzebah."

Not surprisingly, only minutes after drinking the laudanum-laced brew, Olivia fell into a deep, dark abyss.

At some time during the night she awoke. Dawn had not yet added its pink hues to the dark blue of the night sky visible through the window, yet the unnatural quiet of the street below told Olivia that it was well past two or three in the morning. Her thinking was a bit foggy, a result of the medication she supposed, and she decided that the wisest thing she could do was go back to sleep. She was searching for a dry spot on the pillow, one where Esme had not dribbled cold water, when she thought she heard someone in the darkened room.

Normally, she would have called out Esme's or Hepzebah's name, but something stopped her voice—some creepy sensation—and as that sensation worked its way up her spine, it rendered her speechless. *Was someone there*? A darkish form appeared to be standing beside the Davenport desk, but to own the truth, Olivia was not at all certain she was not dreaming.

Again, thanks to the laudanum, her vision was a bit out-of-focus, and when she attempted to move her arms and legs, they refused to obey her commands. Her throat was so dry she could barely swallow; even so, Olivia was certain she could not remain in this frightened state for another moment. With a great effort, she managed to utter, "Who is it?"

The form—be it phantom or human—turned, and Olivia blinked until her eyes were focused enough to see a rather smallish person completely concealed by a voluminous black domino. The silk cape was secured at the neck by a fancy braided rope with tassels at each end, and the hood had been pulled low to obscure the wearer's face. The person held a candlestick containing a mere stub of a candle, and by the meager light Olivia recognized what was in the person's other hand. It was the stack of Jane Frant's poems.

As if guessing what would come next, Olivia found the strength to whisper, "No, please. Do not!"

The words had only just left her lips when the person in the domino touched the candle flame to the papers. The folded sheets caught fire surprisingly fast, and in a matter of seconds the orange and blue blaze had assumed the proportions of a small conflagration.

As if to illustrate the dangers of playing with fire, the flames reached higher, and suddenly one of the tassels at the end of the braided rope was burning. With a high-pitched scream, the intruder dropped the candle and the burning papers on the carpet, then yanked at the the braided rope, dropping it and the domino as well.

Olivia did not see the person flee the room, she was too busy trying to make her body obey her command to get out of the bed. The domino lay in a heap on the floor, and for a moment she thought it had smothered the flames. Unfortunately, she was mistaken, for within moments the flame was back, consuming the dark garment with alarming speed.

Even in her drugged state, Olivia realized that if she did not do something, the deadly flames that were now shooting several feet in the air would soon reach the blue silk bed hangings. If that happened, she would not stand a prayer of escaping with her life.

Struggling to move, she managed to pull herself to the side of the bed, where she reached for the candlestick Hepzebah had set on the bedside table. Grasping the utilitarian pewter, she began to pound with all her might on the wall behind her bed, all the while praying as she had never prayed before.

It was unclear who heard her—heaven or Hepzebah—but the maid was the first to reach the bedchamber. "Lord luv us!" she said, stopping just short of the dancing flames. "What madness is this?"

Ever practical, the servant grabbed a poker from the fireplace and pulled the burning mass of cloth over onto the hearth, where she beat it until it was nothing but a smoking, foul-smelling mass. When she was reasonably confident that the flames would not reassert themselves, she grabbed the bowl of water Esme had left on the bedside table and poured it on the carpet where the burning domino had been.

Convinced at last that every spark had been beaten or doused, she went to the bed and folded a trembling Olivia into her arms. "There, there, Miss Livvy. You've had a right troublesome day, and that's a fact, and as me old pa would say, you've earned a good cry. Truth to tell, I feel a bit shaky myself, for though I never liked this heathen city, I never expected we'd be burned in our beds."

Ten minutes later, all three of the St. Guilford women sat on the rose settee, huddled together for warmth. Because they might all have been killed, Olivia felt she owed it to them to relate the entire

story of her meeting with Denholm Crighton, plus the
chance encounter with his jealous wife, whose uncon-
trolled anger had led her to strike Olivia. "I have
already told Esme about Cousin Jane's correspondence, and the man she loved, but I think you deserve
to hear the story as well, Hepzebah."

Leaving out only a few of the most personal details
Jane had written in her diary, Olivia told them everything. When she was finished, Hepzebah was the first
to speak. "May the good Lord forgive me if I'm
wrong, but I'm thinking 'twere not enough for that
old she-devil to strike you, Miss Livvy. I'm thinking
she came back to finish the job."

"Oh, no," Esme said, "I cannot believe it to be
possible, for even Augusta Crighton could not be that
angry. Why, had you not put out the flames, Hepzebah, we might all be dead by now. Us and half the
guests of the hotel."

"A lot that she-devil would care! Let the gentlemen
believe that women are the weaker sex. Me, I know
better, and I say a scorned female is a very dangerous animal."

"But how could Mrs. Crighton have gained access
to the suite?" Esme asked. "The door was locked, was
it not?"

"Oh, yes," Hepzebah replied, "I locked it myself. I
made sure of it, because just the other night I thought
I heard someone, and—"

"My reticule!" Olivia said. "I forgot all about it. I
must have dropped it in the Crightons' vestibule."

Chapter Fifteen

*N*one of the three women returned to their beds that night, and though they were all shaken by what might have happened, by morning Olivia's fear had turned to anger. Red, hot anger!

She understood jealousy—or she thought she did, it being the emotion that led Cain to murder Abel, his own brother—but how dare someone endanger so many lives!

She had no proof that Augusta Crighton had been the person in the black domino, the person who might so easily have burned Grillon's Hotel to the ground, murdering who-knew-how-many people. Certainly there was not enough proof to have the deranged woman arrested. Even so, Olivia had no intention of letting the incident pass as if it were of no particular importance. If nothing else, she meant to give Augusta a piece of her mind, and she wanted Denholm Crighton to know the extent of the damage wrought by his casual disregard for his marriage vows.

Before she paid one last visit to the Crighton town house, however, there was a letter she must write. A letter to the man she loved with all her heart. It was clear to her now that if she and David Crighton had ever had a chance for a future together, that chance died last night, destroyed in the fire that consumed the copies of Jane Frant's poems.

Be that as it may, Olivia owed David an explanation, and she meant to give him the entire story, from the day she found the poetry and correspondence her cousin had kept hidden in a false drawer in her bedchamber desk, to last night's near catastrophe. Of course, there was every possibility that he would not believe her version of what happened. Family loyalties might prompt him to give the greatest credence to whatever web of lies his aunt and uncle invented to justify their behavior.

No matter which of them he chose to believe, it did not change the fact that Olivia felt she must apprise him of the situation. His conscience and his character would tell him what to do with the information.

Her course of action set, she went to her bedchamber, seated herself at the little cherry Davenport desk, then placed on the green leather-covered top a quill, a pot of ink, and a sheet of velum. After dipping the nib into the ink, she began the most difficult letter of her life.

Dear David,

> *First, allow me to tell you that I love you with all my heart. That said, I will add that I expect nothing from you. My love for you carries with it no obligations, no presumptions, and no expectations of reciprocation.*

Following that confession, Olivia was obliged to pause for several minutes, for her lips had begun to tremble, and she was in eminent danger of raining copious tears upon the page, smudging the words she had already written. It was more difficult that she had imagined to tell a man that she loved him, then in the same breath inform him that she expected nothing from him.

And, of course, it was a bold-faced lie. Naturally she

expected something from him! Expected it. Needed it. Longed for it. Perhaps hers was a fantasy worthy of a children's storybook, but she wanted David to rush to her side the instant he read her letter and assure her with sweet words and even sweeter kisses that nothing and no one in the entire world meant more to him than she.

A fantasy? Yes, but was she not entitled to a few simple words of love in exchange for having given her heart?

Had Cousin Jane asked herself that same question? Had Augusta Crighton?

Though startled by this last thought, Olivia figuratively erased it from her brain. At this moment, the last thing she wanted was to feel sympathy for Augusta.

Convinced that the task of writing this letter would not get any easier with time, Olivia hurriedly told David about the long-distance love affair between Jane and Denholm, then about the incident at Lady White's, and about everything that happened at the town house, leaving out none of Augusta's accusations or actions. Finally, she related the story of the intruder in the black domino and the subsequent fire. After stating her intention of returning to Grosvenor Square to give the Crightons a dressing down they would not soon forget, she concluded with the most difficult paragraph of all.

If you do not love me, or even if you do return my feelings, yet do not wish to be a permanent part of my life, I will not press you. David, you fill my heart with a rapture I thought never to know, but I do not want you unless you can promise me your entire heart and soul. I deserve nothing less.

With sincere wishes for your continued happiness,
Olivia Mallory

After rolling a green baize blotter across the last few lines, she folded the sheet, affixed a wafer, then wrote across the front: *Lord Crighton. The Albany.*

David made good time on his return journey from Kent, having left Crighton Park, his ancestral home near the village of Wexham, at first light. He had just turned his curricle and pair over to one of the Albany's grooms and was about to cross the forecourt when his attention was caught by a man standing on the porch of the red brick building—a man as purposefully nondescript as a little brown wren.

This unprecedented visit by Norman Upjohn encouraged David to hope that the man had learned the identity of the person who had sent the dead cat and the threatening note to his uncle.

"Good morning, Upjohn," he said as soon as they were within speaking distance. "May I ask that you say nothing about your reason for being here until we are abovestairs, in my apartment?"

The man put one blunt-tipped finger across his lips to indicate his willingness to remain silent.

Five minutes later the two men were seated at a drop-leaf table where David often took his meals. The apartment was not large, and privacy was often difficult to achieve with a servant in close proximity, so David asked nothing of his guest until after his valet had brought two tankards of ale, then taken himself off to the small kitchen. "Since I do not delude myself that you are here for the pleasure of my company, Upjohn, I must assume you have something of importance to tell me of my uncle."

"I have something to tell, true enough, my lord. Though what it has to do with Mr. Denholm Crighton and the threats against him, I cannot say, not at this moment."

As was his habit, David reserved all questions and comments until after the man had finished relating everything he had come to say. Unfortunately, when he heard about his aunt's vicious attack on Olivia Mallory, slapping her and nearly knocking her to the ground, he could remain silent no longer. "Damnation! How did this happen? And why?"

"That, I cannot say, my lord. All I can do is relate to you the account of the event as witnessed by my employee, the fellow who is acting as your uncle's temporary footman."

Upjohn had only just finished telling everything he knew when David's valet appeared in the doorway and gave a discreet cough. The servant carried a small silver tray on which reposed a letter. "Beg pardon, my lord, but a footman from Grillon's Hotel just delivered this. He said it was of the utmost importance, and since your lordship has been away from town, I thought I had best bring it to—"

The servant was surprised into silence when his employer rushed forward and snatched the missive from the tray, tearing the wafer and unfolding the single sheet of velum as though it might contain state secrets.

"Good God!" David said, glancing to the end of the page to be certain of the signature. "It is from Miss Mallory, and she must have been in a state of considerable agitation when she wrote the letter, for her penmanship is an absolute scrawl. Very nearly unreadable."

After struggling for several minutes to make sense of that portion of the letter he could read, he pushed the velum toward Norman Upjohn. "See what you can decipher."

Moments later, Upjohn, the battle-hardened operative who had been responsible for more than one French agent disappearing, never to be heard from again, turned a deep shade of red. "The, er, young lady says she loves you, my lord, but that there, er, b'aint any strings to—"

"Not that!" David said. "Go to the second paragraph, where she mentions something about my uncle."

The smaller man returned to his perusal of the letter. "She mentions yesterday's contretemps with Mrs. Augusta Crighton, pretty much corroborating the story I had from my man. Then there is something about . . ." He paused, spelling out a few letters. "L . . . a . . . u . . . d . . . I cannot make out the entire sentence, my lord, but I believe the lady claims that someone gave her laudanum."

Ignoring the younger man's muttered curses, Upjohn continued. "Oh, my. Here in this last bit, sir, Miss Mallory tells of someone stealing into her bedchamber while she slept and setting the room afire."

"Afire! While she slept!" David had not returned to his chair, and now he was obliged to grasp the edge of the table to steady himself.

During the past few years, he had spent more time on enemy soil than at home, and he had faced danger more times than he cared to remember. In fact, less than a year ago, when he had been stabbed and tossed into the River Seine, he had considered himself as good as dead. And yet, none of his experiences had left him feeling as helpless as he felt at this moment, knowing that Olivia had been drugged, and that someone had set fire to her bedchamber.

Just imagining what might have been the outcome of that fire filled him with a fear such as he had never known before. A fear so intense it twisted his insides into knots and very nearly stopped the beating of his heart.

He might have lost the woman he loved before he even realized how much he loved her. Now he wondered why he had not realized sooner just how much Olivia meant to him. She was beautiful, likable, intelligent, and passionate, and in his thirty-one years he had never wanted any woman as much as he wanted her. After their shared kiss he had asked himself if he was the marrying kind. Now, as he realized how close he had come to losing her, he knew that nothing on earth would give him greater pleasure than to spend the rest of his life with Olivia.

As if suddenly gifted with prescience, David knew that their love was the product of destiny—it had begun the moment their gazes met across the hotel lobby—and neither flood, nor hellfire, nor crazed relatives would stop him from marrying Olivia Mallory as soon as legally possible.

"Come," he said to Norman Upjohn, "I must get to Grillon's immediately."

"No need for that," the brown wren said, pointing to a line in the letter. "If I have read this correctly, Miss Mallory may even now be on her way to Grosvenor Square."

"What! Why?"

"To, er, accuse your aunt of attempted murder."

"Of all the—" David groaned like one pained by what he heard. "I beg you, tell me you misread her words. Tell me she did not tempt Fate a second time."

Upjohn did not bother with a reply to that question, nor did Lord Crighton wait for one. They merely looked at each other, speculation in both sets of eyes; then, as if they were of one mind, the two men grabbed their hats and ran from the apartment.

Twenty minutes earlier David had let the groom take his curricle and pair back to the stables, and now he was much too anxious about what might be happening at Grosvenor Square to wait for the horses to be brought around again. He was looking up and down Piccadilly for a hackney when Upjohn informed him that he had come in his gig. "It's just there," he said, pointing to the curb where the street lad he had hired to walk the sweet-mouthed sorrel stood waiting.

Without another word, the two men crowded into the narrow gig, and while Upjohn took up the ribbons,

David tossed the street lad a guinea. With eyes big as saucers, the lad caught the gold coin in midair. He was still shouting his thanks when Upjohn turned the sorrel up Bond Street, then headed at a rather treacherous speed toward Upper Grosvenor Street.

The two men said very little during the short drive, and David spent the time trying to reconcile his image of his shy aunt Augusta with that of a person so unstable she would sneak into an innocent woman's bedchamber and set it afire. Try as he might, he could not do so. Nor could he convince himself that Augusta would send her husband, the man she had loved her entire life, a piece of maggoty meat or a dead cat accompanied by a threatening letter. Such things were totally out of character for such a fastidious woman.

True, his aunt had always been unsure of her husband's affection, but that must be common enough where couples married for convenience; especially when one of the pair had actually given their heart. Once or twice David had spied his aunt in an unguarded moment—moments in which her eyes, her face, her entire countenance had revealed the intensity of the unrequited love she felt for her husband. Naturally, such feelings were fertile soil for jealousy, but nothing David had ever seen had suggested that his aunt was unstable enough to threaten the life of another human being.

David could believe that his aunt, having found proof that her husband had bestowed his affection upon another woman, might send those letters the footman found—the ones containing the single word, "adulterer." Such letters might be her handiwork, but she did not use the flowery sort of language employed in the threatening note. Furthermore, the writer of the note had accused Denholm of stealing something that belonged to him. Or her.

David was still trying to make the pieces of the puzzle fit when Upjohn reined in the sorrel before the town house in Grosvenor Square. "You go on in, my lord. I'll wait here until you send one of the servants out to take my horse."

Not hesitating, David jumped down to the pavement and ran up the stairs to the entrance. To his surprise, the door stood open, and when he pushed it wider still, he found the ersatz footman lying on the floor of the vestibule. The servant's eyes were closed, and blood gushed from his forehead, where he had been struck by something heavy and potentially lethal.

The elderly butler, who sat motionless in a straight-backed chair, had gone so far as to place his handkerchief over the younger man's wound to stanch the flow, but now the blood-soaked linen lay beside the unconscious footman, long forgotten. As for the butler, his wrinkled face was ashen and his lips trembled as they mumbled something unintelligible.

David yanked off his cravat and pressed it against the footman's wound, then he touched the butler's shoulder to gain his attention. Striving to keep his voice even, he said, "Is Miss Mallory here?"

"We should have gone to the country," the butler said. "As soon as that dead cat arrived, we should have taken the knocker off the door and gone someplace safe."

With no time to be gentle, David took the old retainer by the shoulders and gave him a shake. "Answer me, damn you. Is Miss Mallory in the house? And what of my uncle? Is he here?"

"In . . . in the bookroom," the butler replied. "But I would not go in there if I were you, my lord, for Mr. Crighton is not alone."

David suspected as much, and after assisting the servant to his feet and instructing him to go out to the street to tell the man in the gig what had happened, he hurried down the short corridor. The bookroom door was ajar, and though he fully expected to find his aunt there, waving a weapon about while ranting like some sort of lunatic, what he heard stopped him in his tracks. The voice belonged to a man, and that man spoke quietly and with a bone-chilling calm. If anyone was deranged, it was the speaker.

"I will not wait all day," the man said. "The choice is yours, Crighton. Either you write a letter, confessing that you have been stealing from me for years, since our days at Eton in fact, claiming as your own poetry written by me, or I will put a bullet through Miss Mallory's head. A shame, of course, to defile such pretty hair."

For an instant, David could not breathe. He could not think. The woman he loved was in danger, and he did not even know who threatened her.

Fully aware that he would be of no value to anyone unless he kept his wits about him, David took a deep breath, then let it out slowly. Fortunately, while he exhaled, the experience gained from years of dangerous missions inside France came to his aid, and he grew reasonably calm. The man, whoever he was, obviously had a gun, and he had threatened to shoot Olivia. David knew he must stop him, but he knew as well that it would not be in Olivia's best interest to burst through the door like some green recruit with dreams of becoming a hero.

Before taking action, a man with any sense would first determine the extent of the danger. Then, he would pinpoint where all parties involved stood in relationship to the man who presented the threat to their well-being. With these objectives in mind, David tiptoed to the door, then peeked through the narrow opening. What he saw made the blood run cold in his veins.

His uncle stood near the fireplace, and he had drawn his wife very close behind him, using his body to shield her from possible harm. Augusta's face was pressed against her husband's back, and if the shaking of her shoulders was any indication, she was crying.

As for the man with the gun, he stood before the French windows that led to the small back garden. Obviously unmoved by Denholm's chivalrous shielding of his wife, the villain held Olivia in front of him, using her to protect himself.

The blackguard was no more than an inch or so taller than Olivia, so David could not see his face, but it was enough to see the man's left arm wrapped around her slender neck, with his forearm pressing hard against her windpipe. In his right hand was a pocket pistol with an ornately carved ivory handle, and though David was certain Olivia had never done the man any harm, he held the deadly weapon to her temple, his finger on the trigger.

The pocket pistol was the sort with two barrels, with one lock that slid over to fire the second barrel. Though it did not necessarily follow that the villain had loaded both barrels, David was not fool enough to act on that assumption. Not with Olivia's life at stake.

While he tried to think how best to get inside the room without frightening the villain into pulling the trigger, the man spoke again. "You stole my work, you bastard! Then you bamboozled everyone into believing that the poems you claim to have written came from your own brain."

"Good God, man," Denholm said, "you cannot still be holding to that boyhood fantasy that I need any words of yours to create a poem?"

"Liar! Thief! But for you, I might have been famous. Like Lord Byron, I would have been a celebrated poet, one admired by all of society. Instead, most of the *ton* consider me an eccentric with mere delusions of talent. They laugh behind my back, though they think I do not know it. Once I have your confession, however, everyone will be forced to admit that it is I—Arthur Hix—who possesses the God-given talent for poetry, while you are no better than a criminal."

Sir Arthur Hix! David should have guessed as much, for the man had hated Denholm Crighton since their school days at Eton.

"Let Miss Mallory go," Denholm said, "then you and I can talk this matter through."

"Talk it through!" Hix screamed, his voice rising with each word spoken. "That is what you said when I went to the headmaster after you stole 'The Lake.' Do you remember that poem, Crighton? How could you not, for the headmaster had it mounted on a board and hung in the dining hall for all to see."

His uncle said something David did not hear, but if his words were meant to have a calming effect on Sir Arthur, they failed in their purpose.

"Oh, you changed some of the words, right enough," Hix said, his voice filled with scorn, "but you cannot stand there and tell me that you did not steal that poem from my room."

When Denholm made no reply, Sir Arthur cleared his throat, then began to recite the poem in question.

> *I beg for my sake,*
> *You remember the lake,*
> *The blue sky of spring,*
> *The birds on the wing.*
> *If you should forget,*
> *pray have no regret*
> *for I will—*

"Please," Denholm said, contempt in his tone, "there is no need to recite to me your schoolboy drivel. Why, half the boys in the class wrote poems with similar lines, for they are precisely the sort of pap a halfling would write."

"Damnation," David muttered beneath his breath, "keep quiet, Uncle. The man is unhinged. Do not add to his list of grievances."

Quite sure his uncle was not helping the situation, David decided he must do something to ease the tension in the room. Otherwise, Hix might become so rattled that he pulled the trigger without actually meaning to do so.

More than once David had survived a tense situation in which a nervous man seemingly wielded all the power, and his first course of action had always been to allow the fellow to talk without fear of confrontation. Employing an unhurried, friendly voice, David would ply the person with simple yet personal questions. If the man allowed the questions, then answered them, in time a sort of camaraderie would be established between them, and the fellow would begin to let down his guard. Once that happened, David would gradually move in closer, until he was able to disarm the individual without risking his own life or the lives of any innocent bystanders.

Convinced that a similar approach was what was needed with Sir Arthur, David leaned his shoulder against the door frame, assuming an air of nonchalance, then he tapped lightly on the door. Slowly, as if he had nothing better to do, he used the toe of his boot to push open the door. Four pair of eyes were trained on him.

"Sir Arthur," he said, not moving from the doorway, nor changing by so much as an inch his casual pose. "A pleasure to see you, sir. Though you and I have not met previously, Miss Mallory tells me that you are president of a poetical society. How very interesting, for I have always admired poets and poetry. It is a rare gift, the ability to take the most common, ordinary words and put them together so they form a beautiful picture."

Sir Arthur merely stared at David, as if unable to decide what to make of him.

"I have absolutely no talent with words," David

continued, "but I am a most appreciative audience. I believe your society welcomes visitors on Thursday afternoons. Is that not correct?"

"Yes . . . yes, it is," Sir Arthur answered slowly, as if confused by David's manner.

"Wonderful. Then I shall hope to see you there in a few days' time. On Lexington Street, is it?"

Chapter Sixteen

Mistakes. Mistakes. Mistakes. Only yesterday, Olivia had accused herself of making enough blunders this past fortnight to satisfy her lifetime's quota. Unfortunately, returning to Grosvenor Square was proving to be her most deplorable error so far, and with a pistol pressed against her temple, she wondered if this mistake might prove to be her last.

With the wisdom of hindsight, she saw how foolish she had been to come here. The Crightons' butler had thought so as well, and the elderly servant had tried his best to persuade Olivia that his master and mistress were not at home. As well, that very peculiar footman had given it as his opinion that Miss Mallory should return to Grillon's immediately.

Naturally, Olivia had refused to listen to their advice and an argument had ensued. Soon Denholm Crighton had come from his bookroom to investigate the cause for the raised voices in the vestibule. "What is the meaning of this commotion? Can a man find no peace in his own home?"

While both the butler and the footman attempted to justify their part in the disturbance, Augusta Crighton appeared as if by magic from regions unknown. If the malice visible in her eyes was any indication, her anger against Olivia had not abated one iota. "You!" she said, pointing an accusing finger at Olivia. "How dare you return here. You must be insane."

"Now that, madam, is a subject I should like to discuss in further detail. Though I wonder which of us a magistrate might consider unbalanced."

"A magistrate?" Denholm asked. "Surely we need not involve the authorities in our squabbles. What say you, Miss Mallory, that we all adjourn to my book-room where we can discuss the matter like rational—"

Whatever he had meant to suggest, he was never allowed to finish his thought, for at just that moment Sir Arthur Hix pushed his way past the entrance door, which the footman had not closed all the way. And judging by the pistol Hix held in his hand, the idea of a rational discussion did not figure in his plans.

At sight of the weapon, the elderly butler fell back against the wall in a faint, while the footman lunged forward, obviously thinking to take the pistol from Sir Arthur by force. Like many well-laid plans, that one went awry, for Sir Arthur, who had always impressed Olivia as being a bit effete, moved aside with surprising quickness. With a totally unexpected show of viciousness, he swung the arm holding the pistol and dealt the taller, younger man a blow across the forehead.

The astonished footman toppled over like a felled tree, with blood spurting from a deep gash just above his left eyebrow. While he lay on the floor, apparently unconscious, Sir Arthur pointed the pistol at the three who remained standing and ordered them to precede him to Denholm's bookroom.

The ten minutes that followed were like a living nightmare, with Augusta sobbing uncontrollably, afraid her husband would be killed, and Sir Arthur accusing Denholm of every ill—real or imagined—that had ever befallen him. Just when Olivia thought matters could not get any worse, Sir Arthur decided he needed a protective shield, and before she knew what he was about, he grabbed her, pulled her in front of him, and wrapped his arm so tightly around her throat that he very nearly choked off her air supply. The man was stronger than he looked, and though Olivia tried desperately to make him loosen his hold on her, tugging and scratching at his imprisoning arm with all her strength, her efforts brought no positive results.

Fear of asphyxiation left her weak, but it was the pistol pressed against her temple that frightened her so badly her knees began to shake like a blancmange. Only when she heard the soft rap at the door and turned to see David lounging against the doorjamb, looking for all the world as if he had not a care, did Olivia realize that fear had many layers. There was the fear a woman felt for her own safety, then there was that other fear—the one that completely over-shadowed all others—the fear for the safety of the person she loved with all her heart.

Go away, David, she begged silently. *Do not put yourself in harm's way.*

Naturally, he did not go away. In fact, he remained at his ease in the doorway, acting as though Sir Arthur was a guest invited to tea, and not a maniac threatening to do murder. After a series of what Olivia considered inane questions, David straightened from his lounging position and took one leisurely step into the room. Just the one step, no more, and all the time he smiled.

"I have often wondered, Sir Arthur, about that special gift that resides inside the heart and brain of a painter or a poet. Poets and painters," he repeated, shifting his weight from one foot to the other, all the while moving one nearly imperceptible step closer. "What is it that allows you artistic types to see things the rest of us poor mortals are never allowed to see?"

When Sir Arthur did not reply, David shifted his weight again, taking one more step forward. "For instance, when I look into the sky, all I find there is empty space and perhaps a few clouds. When I gaze into the ocean, all I notice is the water. Nothing more. You poets, however, are a breed apart. When you look into the sky or the ocean, you behold a myriad of images. Having perceived those images, you use your skill at words to tell the rest of us what was there all along, had we the vision to see it for ourselves."

What, Olivia wondered, was David doing? Clearly he was using his art of persuasion to convince Sir Arthur that he admired him, that he appreciated his talent as a poet. At the same time, he was working his way ever closer to the man, probably thinking that if he got close enough, he could overpower him and take away the pistol.

The very idea of David taking such a risk caused an oppressive weight to settle on Olivia's heart, but when she thought about it rationally and looked into his eyes, she realized that he knew exactly what he was doing. And why should he not? After all, he had spent years helping to defeat Napoleon, and there was every possibility that this was not the first time he had been in a situation like this.

Deciding that the best chance any of them had to live through this episode was to trust in David and follow his lead, Olivia willed herself to put aside as much fear as humanly possible and give her every thought to being of assistance to David.

As if reading her mind, he took one more step into the room. Unfortunately, this time Sir Arthur must have noticed, for he took a step back, dragging Olivia with him and stopping only when his back collided with the glass of the French windows. "Stay where you are," Hix said, removing the cold, hard pistol from Olivia's temple and aiming it directly at David's heart. "I will shoot, of that you may be certain."

"Oh, I am," David said, the smile still very much in evidence. "If I have learned anything in my thirty-

one years, it is to believe the word of a man holding
a pistol." His facial expression did not change in the
least when he added quite affably, "By the way, Sir
Arthur, do you know my friend, Mr. Norman Upjohn?
If you should care to meet him, he is standing just
behind you, with a very large blunderbuss pointed at
the back of your head."

Everything seemed to happen at once. First, Olivia
heard the sound of breaking glass; then, Sir Arthur
turned slightly, as if to look behind him. His move-
ment was not overt; even so, Olivia decided this was
her one chance to help David. Chancing a crushed
windpipe, she let go of the arm that encircled her neck
and grabbed the barrel of the pistol, using both hands.
Calling upon all her strength, she turned the barrel
until it pointed toward the floor.

The arm around her throat tightened and Olivia felt
herself losing consciousness; still, she did not let go of
the pistol. Nor would she; on that she was determined.
If she forfeited her life, she would not let this madman
shoot David.

At the time, it felt as though she and Sir Arthur
struggled for hours, but it was, in fact, mere seconds
before David charged the villain. With his hands
clutched together to form one giant, uncompromising
fist, he hit Sir Arthur on the side of the head, and
down the villain went, pulling Olivia with him. Her
fall was cushioned somewhat by the thickness of the
carpet, but the instant she landed, she felt a shard
from the broken windowpane nip her earlobe. And
still she held to the pistol.

In the next moment, David caught Sir Arthur by
the collar and lifted him off her, and while he pum-
meled the would-be poet, rendering him senseless,
Olivia lay on the floor gasping for air.

"You're all right now, Miss Mallory," said a voice
she did not recognize. "His lordship has knocked Hix

cold, and the villain's sudden loss of health is such that I doubt he will be threatening anyone for a very long time."

David came to her then, and after kneeling beside her, he reached across her still-prone figure and caught her wrist in an iron grasp. "You can let go the pistol now, my love. You were very brave, and may well have saved my life, but I think it would be best if we let Upjohn have the weapon. I am persuaded it will be safer in the hands of someone who knows a bit about such things."

Olivia was more than happy to relinquish the weapon, and as it happened, she was amply rewarded for her compliance. The instant she released her hold on the pistol, David sat back on his heels and pulled her none to gently into his arms, crushing her against his chest, then kissing her in a manner that quite stole her breath away. Only this time she welcomed the loss. In fact, she decided she would cheerfully forgo breathing forever if David would just continue to hold her close, kissing her and murmuring those sweet words against her lips.

"Oh, my dearest love," he said, forsaking her mouth to rain kisses across her face and down the side of her neck, "my precious gift. I was so afraid Hix would—" He grew perfectly still, then gasped and said, "Damn his eyes!"

David had begun to kiss his way back up to her mouth when his lips found her earlobe and tasted blood. "You are wounded," he said, pushing her away so he could inspect the cut. "I vow I will kill the blackguard for this!"

"No! Do not go," Olivia begged, winding her arms around David's neck to keep him there. "Stay here with me."

"No need to be concerned, my lord," Upjohn said, proffering his handkerchief, "for it's a mere pinprick. Furthermore, if you've settled on killing the one responsible, that would be me. I broke the French window, and I believe it was a piece of that glass that pricked Miss Mallory's ear. Not that she'll be noticing, not a brave young lady like her."

Unwilling to sail under false colors, Olivia informed the nondescript little man that she was no heroine. "In fact," she said to David, happy that he had seen fit to wrap his strong arms around her once again, "the last half hour was the most frightening of my life, and if you do not promise to hold me like this, and not let me go for at least a month, I mean to give way to a fit of the vapors that will make Niobe's tears look like playacting."

"A month?" David asked. "I cannot make such a promise." For just an instant, Olivia's world came to an end, then David smiled, and the look she saw in those dark blue eyes—the look she hoped she did not misinterpret—left her weak with happiness. "I mean to hold you forever, my brave, wonderful girl."

"Forever?"

"Through eternity," he said, gathering her so close she was certain she felt the beat of his heart mingling with hers. "I love you to the depths of my soul, and if I should be obliged to relinquish you for so much as a day, I fear my heart would break."

He searched her face, as if seeking the answer to a question he had not actually asked. Apparently he found the answer he sought, for he touched his lips to hers once again, kissing her so gently, so sweetly that Olivia decided she did not need to hear the question.

Crighton Park, Kent
December 1814

When David Crighton entered his wife's bedchamber that evening he found her sitting at the antique writing desk that had once belonged to his mother, concentrating on finishing the letter she had begun seven days ago and abandoned seven times. "Still searching for the right words?" he asked, stopping behind her chair. Folding back the collar of one of the delicate lace night rails that had been a part of her bride clothes, he placed a lingering kiss on the back of her neck. "Can I be of any assistance, my lady?"

His wife chuckled. "You do not fool me for a minute, my lord, for I know the thing you wish to assist me to do, and it involves climbing into that very comfortable bed over there."

"Climbing? Not at all, my love, for it would give me the utmost pleasure to carry you there. In fact, I should like it of all things."

His beautiful wife gave him a knowing smile that set his blood on fire, then she bid him give her just one more minute. "I have finished the letter at last, and before I do anything else, I mean to place it in the metal box along with Cousin Jane's poems, then lock the box in the bottom drawer of this desk."

"You still believe one of our great-grandchildren will find the box one day, and perhaps see to getting the poems published?"

"That is my hope. By then, enough years will have passed that the story of Jane's and Denholm's love cannot harm anyone."

He knew what she meant, of course, that the story could no longer distress Augusta. "By the way, Livvy, there was a letter from my uncle in the morning post."

"Oh? And how does he like living in Whitby?"

"Very well, indeed. He informs me that he is writing poetry again and that he is not unhappy with his efforts. He said as well that both he and my aunt consider the house and grounds perfect for their needs, and that they have no plans of ever returning to London. He suggests that you may wish to have the town house renovated according to your taste."

Olivia shook her head, causing the lovely reddish-blond curls to move gracefully across her slender shoulders. "Even though Sir Arthur agreed to move to Barbados rather than stand trial for attempted murder, I cannot like the idea of ever returning to Grosvenor Square."

"Then we will sell it, my love, and find another house. One we will fill with nothing but happy memories."

"You are very good, my lord."

"As to that," he said, "put that box away and I will show you just how good I can be."

Even after being married for twelve weeks, three days, and fourteen hours, Olivia still blushed at some of his suggestions. This time, however, she merely chuckled. "Sir, you are a rogue of the first order, making such scandalous remarks to an old married lady."

"To my beautiful bride," he said.

Olivia sighed. "Once you escort Esme down that aisle tomorrow morning, and give her in marriage to Joel Windham, she will be the bride, and I will have to join the ranks of the staid married women."

"Never," he said, "for you will always be my bride."

"And you," she said, "will always be my husband, the man who owns my heart."

Having said this, Olivia put aside the quill she had used to write her letter, closed the ink pot, and walked over to the fireplace to join the man she loved. "And now," she said, twining her arms around his neck, "what was that you were saying about carrying me to bed?"

Epilogue

Crighton Park, Kent
August 1974

"*M*om," Beth Crighton, yelled, bursting into her mother's sitting room, ponytails flying, "you'll never guess what I just found."

"No," her mother replied, looking at the soot smudges on the twelve-year-old's face and hands, "but I venture to say it isn't next to godliness."

The young girl groaned. "Muthurr, must you make pathetic jokes when I'm trying to tell you about something very exciting?"

Lady Willa Crighton put aside the list she had been making of items her oldest daughter, Esme, would need for her first year at Oxford and concentrated on her youngest child, the only one of the present generation to possess the family trait of reddish-blond hair. "Very well," she said, "you have my undivided attention. But I warn you, Beth, that whatever it is you're hiding behind your back, it had better not be something slimy you found at the pond."

When Beth brought her newfound treasure from behind her back, it was nothing more than an old metal box, rusted at the corners and around the keyhole. "You know that old desk that's in the attic, the one with the busted leg and the drawer that won't open?"

"Yes? What of it?"

"Well, I opened that drawer, and I found this box inside. But that's not the best part, Mom, for inside the box is a bunch of old poems and a letter dated December 1814. The handwriting of the letter is hard to read, but from what I can make out, the words tell about the person who wrote the poems. Her name and where she was born, that sort of thing."

Interested at last, her ladyship patted the footstool beside her chair, inviting her daughter to join her. "Let's have a look at your discovery."

Half an hour later, Lady Willa Crighton dried the tears that coursed down her cheeks, put the poems back inside the box, then dialed the number of her cousin in London. "Felix?" she said to the gentleman who answered her call, "Willa here. Are you still dating that skinny blond woman who works for Penguin Publishing?"

"If you mean the *slender* one, old girl, then yes, I am."

"Excellent. Be a dear and ring her up to ask if I may come around to see her. I have some poems written by one of the Crighton ancestors, and I'm quite certain your friend will like them."

About the Author

Martha Kirkland is a graduate of Georgia State University and a lifelong student of classical music. She shares a love of tennis with her husband, and a love of the ocean with her two daughters. As a soldier in the war against illiteracy, she volunteers two afternoons a week as a tutor in a local middle school.